SARA CELI

LUSTING
for Luke

A BILLIONAIRES OF PALM BEACH STORY

Published by Lowe Interactive Media, LLC
Copyright ©2017 by Sara Celi

First Edition: November 2017
Library of Congress Cataloging-in-Publication Data
Lusting for Luke (A Billionaires of Palm Beach Story) / Sara Celi –
1st ed
ISBN-13: 978-1979928458 | ISBN-10: 1979928452

LUSTING
for Luke

A BILLIONAIRES OF PALM BEACH STORY

ONE

Luke

The woman in bed next to me had long legs, creamy skin, a tumble of blonde hair, and no clothes. The blue-silk bedsheet had wrapped around her body, and she slept on her side, curled against me. I didn't know her name.

Lately, I didn't know a lot of their names.

Not that it mattered. These days, the women who kept me company had one purpose, and one purpose only. We fucked. They came. The next morning, they left. Repeat.

One night only. Never more.

Sex was one way to pass the time in Palm Beach, one way to make the loneliness that washed over me at night fade away with the ocean waves. For the last few months—no, make that years—I'd torn through the town's charity circuit and endless line of winter parties looking for *something*. Something to take away the pain. Something to soothe the blisters on my broken heart. And something to make me *feel* again.

One thing remained certain—I hadn't found it. Maybe I never would.

I stared at the woman in my bed. She was pretty in the usual ways, but she also had a tangerine tan, and the light streaming into the bedroom from my window didn't do her face any favors. Just like most Palm Beach socialites, she thought nothing of a visit to the Botox fairy, and it showed in the manmade tightness of her face. When the alarm on my iPhone buzzed, I nudged her until she opened her eyes.

What a relief. She'll be leaving soon.

"Good morning." I punched the dismiss button to silence the incessant sound on the device.

She yawned, and I noticed the trace of dark lipstick that still rimmed her mouth. It complemented the mascara smudges beneath her eyes and the shininess on her nose. She wasn't as pretty in the morning as she had been in the moonlight. "Good morning to you, too. What time is it?"

"Seven forty-five."

"Early."

"Sort of."

This woman had a European accent I couldn't quite place…Slovenian? Estonian? Hungarian? I flipped through my hazy memories of the previous night. It started out with a steak dinner at Meat Market, then a meeting with friends from Manhattan for late-night drinks at HMF, the bar inside The Breakers Resort. By then, I'd been too drunk to drive, so I'd taken a taxi home.

Had I met her at HMF? At Meat Market? Had she been with me in the car?

She propped herself on one elbow. "Last night was amazing." Each word she spoke had a crisp, clipped cadence.

"It…it was."

There, that sounds good.

I got out of bed. My boxers lay on the floor along with my black trousers and gray, button-down shirt. I slipped on the shorts and padded to the three-quarter bathroom located just off the master bedroom. "I'm glad you had a good time." I turned on the faucet and splashed cool water on my face. How many times had I slept with this woman?

Damn it.

I needed to tone down the tequila, and probably alcohol in general. Always made the next morning too fuzzy. I knew better than to let my drinking get out of control. Lately, though, I'd been ignoring my own better judgment.

That had to stop, too.

Her hand slipped around my stomach and traveled up my chest. "So? What do you think about meeting up later tonight?"

I grabbed her fingers and turned around. "Not tonight. I've got plans."

Her face fell, and it occurred to me once again that I didn't care if I disappointed her. She needed to leave, and soon.

"You promised we'd have dinner tonight."

"I did?"

"Right before you made me come three times."

"Three?"

Impressive, even for me.

She nodded. "And you said there would be more where that came from."

I moved away from the sink and back into the bedroom. "Listen, I'm sorry, but last night I said a lot of things I didn't mean." I picked up her black dress, which lay on the floor near my discarded loafers. "We had a good time. Let's leave it at that."

"You're kidding."

I didn't reply. Instead, I shot her what I hoped was a bland, no-I'm-not-kidding look.

"My girlfriends told me you were like this."

"Like what?"

"Cold, closed off. No one gets near you." Sighing, she snatched her dress from my hand. "I should have listened to them." She wrapped the stretchy fabric around her body, found her underwear on the floor, and threw it in her straw purse.

"I don't do...relationships," I explained, probably more begrudgingly than I should have let on. The word "relationship" tasted metallic and foreign in my mouth. "Not anymore. Haven't for a while."

I didn't usually offer this kind of explanation, but something about the weariness in her voice made me open a little. Yes, I had a reputation. I knew it. Owned it.

"Everyone in Palm Beach knows what you're like, Luke."

"Then you know that I don't do commitment. It's just not my thing."

"Someday, it will be." She eyed me. "Because you can't keep living this way. No one can. Don't you think that Faye—"

"I think your shoes are downstairs. And I have a meeting at nine."

Wrong. I had a 9:00 AM tee time at the Everglades Club. Not a meeting. But last night's flavor didn't need to know that, and she didn't need to pry into my personal life, either. She stared at me for a moment, and I wondered if she wanted me to flinch, or to change my mind.

"Fine," she finally said. "I'll go."

Less than ten minutes later, she disappeared in a cloud of perfume, disappointment, and confusion. They always did.

TWO

Natalie

"Have you seen this?" My aunt Helen walked around the reception desk at Yoga Ohm, the studio she owned, and handed me her phone. The screen showed me the Facebook event page she'd been focused on for the last few weeks. "Five *hundred* online RSVPs." She grinned. "Five hundred. Can you believe that? This is going to be huge."

I scrolled through the invite page. Already, several dozen commenters had posted in the discussion section. "Wow. Activists from all over the area are coming." I peered up at her again. "Even some from Miami."

She nodded. "A bunch of them. People from all over South Florida."

For the last year or so, protests and marches had been happening every weekend in downtown West Palm Beach. Suddenly, community activism was in vogue, and Helen hadn't wanted to waste a second of that. She'd spent the last two months organizing this march, which would center on equal pay and women's rights. She called it the second most important thing she'd ever done.

My aunt snapped her fingers. "By the way, that reminds me, have you heard from Karen?"

"She's on her way. Texted her this morning, right after she left Kissimmee."

"Excellent. So glad she's coming."

"She's lucky she got off work."

Karen, my mom and Helen's older sister, still lived in the house where I grew up, in a neighborhood of 1950s ranch homes in the not-as-desirable end of Kissimmee. Life for her, and me, had always included a decent amount of struggle. Even after twenty years, she had no idea when she'd be able to quit her job as a radiology tech at Osceola Regional Medical Center. Still, she tried not to dwell on it. "At least I can see the fireworks from Disney World," mom often said whenever she admitted that the house, and her life, weren't as great as she had hoped. "Better than nothing."

Helen was fifteen years younger than my mom. She left central Florida right after high school, drove south, enrolled at the University of Miami, and never looked back. Now, she owned Yoga Ohm, and she'd been kind enough to give me a job after my own graduation from the U, when I hadn't been able to find full-time work marketing work in Miami.

I owed her a lot, and we both knew it.

"So, she'll be here around seven tonight?" I handed the phone back to Helen.

"Maybe a little after."

"Perfect." I glanced at the computer behind the reception desk. We had about fifteen minutes until I needed to teach our 2:00 PM yoga class, a mix of billionaire wives and stay-at-home moms with thousand-dollar investments in the latest athleisure apparel. That day's class had ten less students than usual, though. "Listen, do you think we should be worried about enrollment? Just seems like we've been a little light lately."

"I'm not worried."

"You're not?"

My aunt shrugged. "These things happen from time to time. The students always come back."

"I know, but…" I took a moment to regroup my thoughts. "It just feels like I'm noticing a trend."

The implication hung in the silence between us.

"I know you're still upset that I cut your days back from five to four last week." Helen sighed, and defeat shook in every word she spoke. "Like I told you then, it's just temporary."

"I hope so."

My thoughts turned to the electric bill at my apartment, which I had already gone a month without paying. I couldn't do that much longer, and I also had to make my student loan payment. Those two bills alone wouldn't leave much breathing room for the rest of my expenses.

Maybe I should get a second job as a barista…

"I promise, sweetie. As soon as I can give you a few more hours, I will." Helen picked up her black gym bag from the block of cubbyholes that lined the wall behind the desk. A "The Future is Female" sticker still adorned the side pocket, but the edges had begun to curl away from the fabric. I wondered what she'd do once the sticker finally fell off the bag. "You're okay here the rest of the afternoon? I have so much stuff to do."

"I've got it handled. No problem."

"Great. Thank you so much. I can always rely on you." She tossed her phone into the bag then leaned forward to give me a hug. "And don't forget, I need you to be there at seven thirty tomorrow for setup."

"I won't forget," I said as she pulled away.

"Perfect. You're the best, Natalie."

Helen disappeared through the front door and got into her black Toyota Corolla at the far end of the parking lot. Once she drove away, I turned back to the list of women signed up for our 2:00 PM class. The first ones in this class of eleven would arrive soon. I knew most of them, right down to the small details, like the fact that Jennifer only drank French sparkling water, Gretchen drove a Mercedes G-Wagen, and Yvette had four children she refused to put on anything but a low-carb, vegan diet. I also suspected more than a few things about them, too. Their thin bodies and chemical-peeled faces gave them away.

These women had it easy. So easy.

They were upper-class, white, pampered women who didn't have to worry about anything beyond what time the nanny would arrive, and what dress they'd wear to a fundraiser. Women who would spend eons of their lives making sure that they'd stay well preserved.

Those kinds of women.

The front door jangled, and Gretchen walked through wearing skin-tight yoga pants, silver loafers, and an oversized green top. She breezed up to the reception desk and removed her gold sunglasses. Her long, brown ponytail wrapped partially around her shoulder.

"Oh, gracious, Natalie," she said through her professionally whitened teeth. "You have no idea how glad I am to see you. Traffic is a nightmare already." Her eyes widened, and she handed me a keychain with our studio membership tag attached to it. "It's a disaster. I hate season, don't you? So many snowbirds."

She couldn't have sounded snobbier if she'd tried.

"A lot of people are in town this year." I swiped the tag through our system and tried my best to keep my expression stoic. I knew better than to engage too deeply with our clients. Best to keep our conversations on the superficial. Anything else could be bad for business. Keep the clients happy, and we'd stay happy, too. I turned to the computer screen and clicked through Gretchen's account, checking her in for the day. She had an unlimited pass to our studio, and usually attended classes three times a week.

"*And* the Southern Bridge is going to be a nightmare this weekend, too. That traffic is as bad as New York City. You've been to the city, haven't you?"

I flinched. "No, I haven't."

In twenty-five years of living, I'd only traveled outside of Florida once—a weekend trip to my uncle's funeral in Chicago. It had been cold, rainy, and forgettable, not unlike so much else in my life.

"Well, you must go." Gretchen dropped her large Louis Vuitton bag onto the lip of the reception desk and rooted around inside it. She produced a white business card, which she handed to me. "That's Pierre at the Four

Seasons Hotel downtown. Call him when you go, and tell him you know me. He'll give you a great deal."

"Thank you," I said as I took the card. I didn't have the heart to tell her that I would never go, and could only guess how much a room at that hotel would cost.

"Meanwhile, I hope that they get that bridge construction done, and soon. I am *so* tired of sitting in traffic for half an hour just to get somewhere." She sniffed. "I even told Samuel that this weekend we can stay in West Palm for dinner—even if it means eating at a fast food restaurant, for god sakes."

I gave her a fake laugh. She'd rather die a death by a thousand cuts than be seen in a place known for things like combo meals, oversized hamburgers, and salty French fries. "Do you think a lot of the others will be late?"

"Oh, I'm sure of it." Gretchen pulled her bag closer to her body. "I'm going to get ready for class. See you in there."

"See you in there."

She headed in the direction of the changing room, and once she disappeared, I sighed. I just didn't have anything in common with the women who frequented the studio, and the last few months had proven it. Still, I needed them. We needed them. Without them, I couldn't come close to paying my bills. I bit the inside of my bottom lip. Something good needed to happen. I needed a break. *We* needed a break.

Soon.

"Ladies and gentlemen!" Two days later, Helen stood in the center of the Meyers Amphitheater with a large megaphone in one hand. "We gather here right now to say that we are united! We are together in this fight!"

The crowd cheered. From my vantage point, it seemed like almost a thousand people had showed up for the rally, and they covered the park lawn, leaving almost no green space. Many of them carried homemade signs, and the best of those had snappy slogans like, "A woman's place is in the resistance" and "My daughter will know she's more than just a pussy" and "Brains over bodies." I held one myself; it said, "Female rights are human rights."

"What do we want?" Helen's scratchy voice echoed over the megaphone.

"Equality!" The crowd roared back the familiar call-and-response cheer.

"When do we want it?"

"Now!"

My mom turned to me. From behind oversized black sunglasses, she said, "I'm so proud of Helen. This is a great statement. She's really done it."

"She *should* be proud."

"Absolutely."

Aunt Helen wasn't like me. She felt things. She knew things. She had conviction. And she had hope that life would get better, that the future could be brighter than the past.

I admired her for all of it.

"We can't march to city hall, like we had originally planned, because of the traffic." Helen still dominated the crowd. "But that doesn't mean we can't command attention and make a statement. From here, we're going to travel a short distance up and down Flagler, and make our voices heard to those who would pretend we don't exist—those who would continue their barbaric and cruel practices! Those who would keep us from our pursuit of justice and equality for all Americans!"

The crowd cheered some more as DJ Freeze, a celebrity performer from South Beach, chimed in with perfectly timed music. Soon, the marchers had set off on their route. We were all together. Focused. Fighting for our beliefs. Nothing in the world could get in our way.

Nothing.

"You did an amazing job." I tossed a few pieces of trash into a garbage bag and hugged Helen. We'd returned to the amphitheater to clean up after the march, and her flushed cheeks magnified her bright eyes. "You should be *so* happy."

She pulled away from me. "The police said they counted over 1200 people. Twelve hundred. Can you believe that? It's one of the biggest rallies they've had in West Palm Beach all winter season."

"They'll force us to make this an annual event if you're not careful."

She grinned. "I couldn't have done this without you."

"Thanks." I smiled back at her. "I think we're about cleaned up here."

"Almost. One more bag or so." She gestured at my mom, also cleaning trash about two dozen yards away. "Do you want to go to lunch with us after this? Your mom mentioned Rocco's Tacos on Clematis."

"She never met a margarita she didn't like." I glanced at my watch. It was 12:13 PM. Because of the rally, we had canceled all the classes at the studio that morning, and didn't have one until five. "What the heck? We've got a couple of hours."

"I'll go tell her the plan."

As she took a few steps away from me, I remembered that I needed to pick up an order at the local grocery. "Aunt Helen—hold on."

She turned back to me.

"I've got to get something at the store. I'll meet you there."

"Can you get it later?"

I shook my head.

"Are you sure? We can wait for you."

"No. Let me put this bag in the dumpster." I pointed across the lawn. "And I'll meet you at the restaurant. I'll be less than five minutes behind you."

The Publix supermarket pharmacy had my birth control prescription waiting, and twenty minutes later, I slipped it into my purse as I stepped outside the store. It wouldn't take long to walk to Rocco's Tacos, and I welcomed the chance to clear my head. Despite my aunt's successful rally, I still had worries pooling in the pit of my stomach. When I'd looked at my budget that morning, I still had a five-thousand-dollar balance on a credit card with no plan to pay it off anytime soon. Two letters in the mail the day before had told me that my insurance company planned to drop out of the Florida health insurance exchange, and my landlord wanted to raise my rent when the lease came up in two months. I also only had $231.66 saved of my $450 student loan payment.

Not good.

I desperately needed a way out of this mess, and I didn't know where to find one. I couldn't ask my mom to help me—her job at the hospital didn't give her much breathing room. Taking even fifty dollars from her would make me feel awful. And with things tight at the yoga studio, I couldn't ask Helen for a raise or extra shifts, either.

There was something so irrevocably shitty about being screwed and knowing it.

As I walked to the restaurant on some of the less-traveled side streets of downtown West Palm Beach, I pulled my phone out of my cross-body bag, opened my banking app, and checked the account balance. I hoped to find more in there than I saw that morning. No luck. No miracle. No rescue.

Still a measly three hundred fifty bucks—

"Hey! Watch where you're going!"

THREE

Natalie

Tires screeched, and a horn sounded. I looked up from the phone and leaped backward. A white McLaren stopped in the street just inches away from me, less than a half second or so from colliding with my left knee. A breath caught in my throat, then I scrambled onto the uneven sidewalk.

The man behind the wheel stopped the car then stepped out of it. "I'm so sorry. Jesus, I—"

Our eyes met...then broke contact and we studied one another. He wore a pair of tan pants, sandals, a gray polo shirt, and aviator sunglasses. Even before he took off the shades, I knew this would be one of the most gorgeous men I had ever seen. And in the last few years, I'd seen a lot of good-looking men float in and out of South Florida.

"Are you okay?" He walked a few steps toward me.

"I-I don't know—" The words caught in my throat, so I took a few gulps of air.

My miniscule bank balance had distracted me so much that I'd wandered off the sidewalk and into the street—against traffic. I put another half foot between the white sports car and me. Between *him* and me.

"I just—oh, my god. I'm so sorry!" the man said with a tone of alarm. "But I didn't hit you, did I?"

I thumped my chest with the heel of my hand. "No, no, I-I'm fine."

"You're sure?"

"Yes." I tried once again to slow down my ragged breaths. I could have hurt myself, or died. "Luckily. You stopped just in time."

"I'm glad you didn't get injured." He took off the designer eyewear and moved closer, giving me a full view of his flawless tan, hooded eyes, and wavy black hair. "That wouldn't have been good. Wouldn't want that."

"You wouldn't?"

I glanced down at the car. A personalized license plate adorned the front, and the glossy vehicle headlights reminded me of cat eyes. How much did these types of cars cost? A hundred thousand? Two? A half million? A minor scratch probably cost ten grand. Yikes.

"*I wouldn't* want to damage your car," I said. "I can't imagine the bills—"

"You mean you don't have universal damage insurance? I thought everyone did."

I frowned. "Damage insurance?"

"Yes, of course. You don't have a policy? It's the law in the state of Florida."

"Is it?" I recoiled. Universal damage insurance? What was he talking about? Was this something else to add to my long list of expenses? "Is that a new thing?"

"Brand new."

My face fell. "Oh, I hadn't heard about it—"

His deep chuckle interrupted me. "Don't worry. I'm joking. It's a joke. I promise."

"A joke?" A pulse of relief pushed through me. "Oh, right. A *joke*. You're kidding."

"What? You don't get it?" He shoved a hand in his pants pocket and his gaze met mine. "My apologies. Sometimes I forget that others don't share my sense of humor."

"No... I'm glad..." I couldn't help but smile at him. "You just caught me on a bad day. I'm not thinking straight."

"Really? This is Palm Beach in February. It's seventy-five degrees and sunny. Every other place in the US is a popsicle compared to here, so how could you be having a bad day?"

"Real life doesn't stop because of the weather. I just... I've had a lot on my mind lately."

"Don't we all?" He paused. "Were you at the march earlier?"

"Yes. How'd you know?"

He pointed at the top of my head. "You're still wearing your hat."

"Oh, god, I forgot to take this off." I ripped the pink, pussycat-shaped cap off my head. A knitting club from Jupiter had given them out to marchers as they arrived at the amphitheater that morning. I hadn't even noticed how hot it made my head. Embarrassed, I shoved it into the Publix plastic shopping bag.

The man's gaze hadn't strayed, and the way he looked at me sent a delicious shiver up my spine. Whoever this guy was, he had a knack for commanding attention.

"Anyway," he said after a beat, "if you're fine, I'll let you get back to whatever you were doing."

I gestured in the direction of Clematis Street. "I absolutely can't keep the margaritas waiting any longer."

"Margaritas?"

"At Rocco's Tacos. Saturday Funday. Gotta pregame for… Sunday Funday." I silently cursed myself. Leave it to me to sound like an idiot in front of Mr. I'm-Too-Sexy-With-My-Aviators.

"Saturday and Sunday Fundays, huh? Wouldn't want anything to get in the way of weekend fun like that." A wry smile crossed his face, and he took a few steps backward. "You know, that restaurant is not far from here. Why don't I drive you?"

My mouth dropped open before I could stop myself, and he laughed again. "I'm not a serial killer or anything like that. I'm a nice guy." He leaned a little closer to me. "Some of the time."

My stomach twisted, but I liked the way it felt. I also loved the way he smelled, which reminded me of cedar and cherries. If I let it, the scent would intoxicate me. "I'm sure you are."

"You can trust me." He opened the passenger door of the car. "So? Why don't you get in?"

Hitching a ride with a guy I'd just met wasn't something I normally did, but what could I say? I'd never seen anyone this hot in West Palm Beach. Ever. I couldn't have turned down this offer if I'd tried.

"Thank you."

I slipped into the seat and ignored the faint warning signs going off in my head, the ones any woman should heed when getting in a car with a stranger. But the soft, red leather beckoned to me. It kissed my legs and enveloped me in instant luxury when I slid across the cool, smooth surface. I'd only seen cars like this from a distance. As the man made his way to the driver side, I took in the small details on the car console, and noticed his gold iPhone resting in the cup holder between the two front seats.

"I'm Luke," he informed me as he climbed in the car and shut the door. "Luke Rothschild." He revved up the engine and held out his right hand. "Pleased to meet you."

"Likewise." I shook his strong hand, and by then, any misgivings I might have had were pacified by his warm grip. "And I'm Natalie. Natalie Johnson."

Luke grinned at me one more time before he accelerated the car.

Anyone driving a McLaren with the last name Rothschild had to be at least a millionaire. Everything about this guy screamed "rich," but that wasn't what kept me stealing glances at him as he drove the few blocks to the restaurant. I kept thinking about the slight hint of a New Yorker's accent in his voice and the way his eyes seemed to see right into my soul when he looked at me.

Sexy. *Damn* sexy.

So, when he steered the car onto Clematis Street, my heart sank a little. Not much time left with this hunk of a man.

"This is it," I announced as the Rocco's Tacos sign came into view. "Where I get out."

"Make sure you get the guacamole." He signaled and parked the car in an open on-street spot. "It's out of this world."

"Agreed. It's my favorite. It's not the typical diet of a yoga instructor, but maybe I'll make this my cheat meal."

"You're a yoga instructor?"

I nodded.

"So, you're an expert at downward dog?" His gaze captured mine for another moment, and my stomach flipped again.

"Yes," I managed. "An expert."

"I'll have to remember that."

My breath caught in my throat. I didn't want to leave the car. I didn't want to leave this man's sight.

"I'm also great at toppling tree. I have a lot of balance."

"That's always been a hard position for me." Luke's gaze roamed my body. "Well, Natalie, the yoga instructor, have a good afternoon."

"You, too."

I couldn't delay any longer. Time to get out of the most expensive sports car I'd ever been in and leave behind its intoxicatingly handsome owner. I hooked two fingers into the latch and opened the door.

"Goodbye," I murmured.

"Goodbye."

Once I stepped out of the car and shut the door behind me, Luke put his sunglasses on again and drove away in the direction of Palm Beach. I was alone, standing there, a normal twenty-five-year-old woman once more.

FOUR

Luke

Picking up random women on the side of the street wasn't a habit of mine, but so what? Lately, the usual hadn't been working; no one knew that more than me. Besides, Natalie had a way about her—an aura, almost—that made her interesting. Plus, a little chivalry never hurt anyone, and I was out of practice.

Truth told, I liked having Natalie in my car more than I expected I would.

In fact, I was still thinking about her a few days later while I tried to finish out a quick round of eighteen holes on the golf course.

"So, I'm thinking. I have a new IPO I'd like you to invest in." Aaron Shields, my closest friend on Palm Beach, took a swing at the ball with his club, and it sailed through the air. He winced as it landed on the edge of the green. "Damn, this is not my day." He turned back to me.

"Kinetic Strategy Fund is doing well. Actually, better than I expected."

"That's great."

"And I wanted to talk with you about doubling down. We should buy some more shares. It's outperforming, and had a 12 percent return last month."

"Great."

"So, you're in for more?"

"That's fine."

"We're talking about an investment of about 350 grand, or so. I think there's a decent chance of gains like what we've been seeing—I might even double your money."

"Whatever you say."

Aaron braced himself against his golf club. "You sure?"

"Yep."

He gave me a meaningful look. "You know what, buddy? You've been a lot quieter than normal. Something bothering you?"

I pulled a golf ball from the pocket of my pants and walked up to the tee. "Nothing's wrong. I'm good."

"Bullshit. This is our second round on the links at Everglades in a week, and you're not enjoying it. *Everglades*, for Christ sakes. It's the best, most exclusive course in Palm Beach County." Aaron put a hand on his hip. "So, tell me what's up."

"It's complicated."

"Everything's complicated when it comes to you."

Aaron had known me for fifteen years. For the last five, he'd managed the investment portfolio that contained the remains of my trust fund and the few million I'd made after college in a short stint as a venture capitalist in Silicon Valley. I considered him my best friend, and he was one of the few who ever saw the real me. I also owed him a lot, and he never let me forget it.

"You might be a Rothschild," he often said. "But that doesn't mean you don't need a shield."

Aaron had a certain way with words. And men. He also loved Palm Beach more than I did. "All the women here look like Patsy from *Absolutely Fabulous*," he'd told me once. "It's a gay man's heaven." Aaron made his way from New York to South Florida as often as he could during the winter, and he spent most of his evenings escorting the town's aging ladies to charity balls and fundraising dinners. Even at forty-two, he still looked decent in a tuxedo.

"The other day, I met someone," I said as I watched the golf ball I'd just hit soar across the golf course. Another wide shot. At this rate, I'd be lucky to make par. "A woman."

"Hold on." Aaron held up a hand. "You never talk about the women you meet, or the ones you sleep with. Ever."

"Nope. But I like this one. And, I didn't sleep with her." I decided to leave out the fact that I hadn't stopped thinking about this woman since I'd watched her disappear into Rocco's Tacos. "She almost ran into my car. That's how we met."

"The McLaren?"

I nodded.

"Oh, god, she didn't scratch it, did she?" Aaron's mouth lifted into a half-smile that highlighted the crow's feet around his eyes. "That would be a shame."

"No, she didn't damage it. She was…cute. Natalie… something. She'd been at the women's march downtown."

"The women's march? For god sakes, when is this protesting going to stop?" Aaron shuddered. "It's such an ugly look for people. I can't even go on Instagram any-more. People are protesting *there*, of all places. Every oth-er post is this or that—"

"They have legitimate beefs."

"But it's so *boring*. If they keep this up, they're going to have to protest the whole world."

"Says the guy who marched in New York the day they overturned same-sex marriage at the Supreme Court."

"You know I support gay rights. Transgender rights. Women's rights. All of it. I'm just saying…" Aaron spread his hands. "Protesting works, but at some point, you have to live your life."

"Speaking of living…we have a hole to finish." I set off toward the golf cart, and Aaron followed me. Before I got into the driver's seat, I said over my shoulder, "Oh, and by the way, she works out at Yoga Ohm. Maybe even teaches there. She had their logo on her shirt."

I'd noticed other things about her, too, like the way her black ankle pants showed off her curves, the small flecks of green in her blue eyes, and the spray of moles that danced across her upper chest, inviting me to look closer.

But I didn't need to share that with Aaron.

"You're really interested in her, aren't you?" My friend eyed me. "Perhaps this one is different?"

"Maybe." I shrugged. "What if she is?"

"How old is she?" Aaron asked.

"Twenty-five? Twenty-three? I can't tell ages."

Aaron laughed. "Oh, that's rich. A millennial feminist, if there is such a thing. If you start dating her, your father is going to love that."

My father had been married four times, and his latest wife was thirty-two. He was seventy-five, and the years of steak, martinis, and little exercise had begun to affect his health.

I narrowed my eyes at the sound of his name. "Don't bring him up."

"You know what I think about it—I've told you a thousand times. You're wealthy now, but you could be a billionaire. *Billionaire.* All you must do is settle down permanently and take over your father's company. Simple."

I laughed. We both knew my father's definition of settling down included marrying a woman with the *right* last name and the *right* family tree.

"What? People have done far more for far less."

"I know—"

"Do you?" Aaron cocked his head. "You've been down here for almost two years, nursing a broken heart and avoiding your birthright. Honestly, man, you can't keep obsessing over the same woman. This self-imposed exile of yours is getting pretty stale."

"I'm not obsessing over Faye."

Aaron let out a rueful laugh. "You are. It's more than just grief." His eyes softened. "We all loved her, and we miss her. But don't you think—"

"You know I took all of that"—I waved a hand— "all of that mess pretty hard."

"I know you did. Anyone would." He clapped a hand on my shoulder and pulled me close. "But you're turning thirty-five in a month, my friend, and you have to face that. It's happening, whether you want it to or not."

It was. I knew that full well.

"Listen, everyone knows that your dad wants to stop running the business and retire in Greenwich. And he wants you to be at the helm of the company." Aaron released my shoulder, walked over to the golf cart, retrieved his water bottle, and crossed back to the other side of the green. He nodded. "With a woman from a certain kind of family."

"Still can't believe he made me sign that ridiculous contract."

"Neither can I, but he did. You know how obsessed he is about you carrying on the family name. He's always wanted to build a dynasty, and he wants it done before he's too old to enjoy it." Aaron eyed me. "Maybe this… Natalie…is worth considering? Anybody is, at this point."

He didn't need to remind me. I had thirty days left to find someone who my father would accept.

"Dad wants me to marry a New York blueblood. Not a yoga teacher from South Florida."

"You could always make up a backstory about her. Make her a long-lost aristocrat from Europe." Aaron sipped some water. "But that's also the loophole. He didn't specify the *type* of woman you had to marry when you signed that paperwork."

I bristled at the word "paperwork." I'd been just twenty-five when I agreed to his terms, and fresh out of Harvard Business School with an MBA in my hand. I'd wanted so badly to please my father, and at the time, his conditions hadn't seemed so bad. But that was almost ten years ago. And long before Faye.

"Like I said." I raked a hand through my hair. "I'm pretty sure that Natalie is barely legal."

Aaron cocked his head. "You're still young. Don't they say thirty-five is the new twenty?"

"No one has ever said that." I laughed. "Besides, I'm not thirty-five yet."

"Okay. *Thirty-four* is the new twenty."

"I also never said she liked me."

"You're Lucas Rothschild." He shook his water bottle at me. "She will. They always do."

Aaron's words—or possibly the violent way he brandished that bottle at me—jolted me back to thinking about my agreement with my dad. Aaron's present chatter faded and became replaced by his earlier words…

You're turning thirty-five in a month, my friend, and you must face that.

But that's also the loophole. He didn't specify the type *of woman you had to marry when you signed that paperwork.*

I blinked. Blinked again and again, propping the driver behind my neck and across my shoulders. I rolled the cool metal up and down my neck. Relief flooded my gut as the ideas started to flow.

My mind worked at mega speeds, crafting the solution to all my problems, right there on hole number sixteen.

Aaron finally shut up and shot me an odd look. He grabbed my arm and drew me back, so a group of boisterous men could play through. At that point, I didn't care. I was grinning so big, my face hurt.

"*Yes*, that's it," I mumbled under my breath, and then I tossed my golf club up in the air. Golfers ducked, and Aaron cussed like a sailor, but I laughed. Giddy, I was so damn giddy it wasn't even funny.

Yeah, *that* was the moment I must have gone completely crazy.

I hadn't done the lotus pose or toppling tree in forever. A few months after Faye died, and at the bottom of my pit of grief, I dated a yoga enthusiast named Margaret who grew up in Brooklyn and claimed to be best friends with one of JD Salinger's distant relatives. The sex had been fantastic, but that was about it. Margaret had always called yoga the "key to a healthier you," and she cajoled me for weeks until I finally agreed to try a class with her one afternoon. Once I started, she didn't let me stop, and for about six months, I contorted and twisted my body into every pose she wanted, hoping that would make up for our lack of chemistry outside the bedroom.

It didn't.

When I finally ended it with her, she'd said a version of the same thing that almost all the women in my life ended up saying: "You're lost. No one can fix you; you have to fix yourself."

I hadn't stepped foot in a yoga studio since.

Still, that didn't mean I couldn't try it again, and I'd been meaning to add something to my usual six-mile runs and spinning classes. What harm could a little downward dog do?

After golf and lunch with Aaron at Taboo on Worth Avenue, I drove back to my beach house and found an ancient blue workout mat stuffed behind some tennis rackets and a broken golf club in the utility closet of the garage. I changed into a pair of sweatpants and a t-shirt, switched the McLaren for my less flashy, more sensible BMW sedan, and set out for Yoga Ohm. A quick Google search on my phone showed me the address, phone number, and class schedule on the business Facebook page. If I hurried, I could make the three forty-five "Intro to Hot Yoga" class.

And why the hell not? At the very least, I had a blind shot at finding out more about Natalie Johnson and her pink, knitted hat. Not a horrible way to spend an afternoon.

Yoga Ohm sat in the center of a strip mall on the ragged edge of Belvedere Road in the southern part of West Palm Beach. A few galleries and a coffee shop rounded out the converted space, which appeared to be the best thing about this neighborhood. I shuddered, parked my car in the back part of the lot, grabbed my mat, and headed toward the door.

"What are you doing here?" Natalie spoke before I did, right as I pushed through the entrance, and about a nanosecond after I recognized her behind the reception desk.

"Hoping to take a class."

Her eyes widened. "Really? Here?"

"Decided it was time to brush up on my skills." I glanced around the small lobby, which had a few benches, some studio-branded apparel on a few racks, a table full of brochures about classes, and a large bulletin board with advertisements about yoga trips and certifications. I had to admire the clean simplicity of the whole place, and the fact that she had enough business savvy to make it her own. "Is this your place?"

"It's my aunt's. I just work here."

"Nice. Cool place. She should be proud of herself."

"She is."

Natalie had her eyebrow raised, and a smile pulled at her lips. "I've been working here about eighteen months. I'm the assistant manager." She leaned against the reception desk. "So how did you find us?"

"It was on your shirt the other day. The one you had on in the car."

"Oh." She looked down at herself; she wore a similar colored top, only this time it had the studio name in faded letters and accented with what appeared to be a tie-dyed sports bra. "It was?"

"Front and center. Good advertising." I crossed a little farther into the crisp lobby. "And I've been wondering. How much are classes?"

"It depends. We sell them in blocks of ten, or as a monthly unlimited membership. But your first class is free."

I placed my mat on the nearest bench. "Looks like I'm here for my first one, then."

She glanced in the direction of what I guessed to be the main practice room. "Well, you'll have to wait. You're late."

"What? It's only three forty-two. Class hasn't started yet."

She nodded. "But we have a strict policy here. Students need to be in place and ready to go when the class begins. There's too much paperwork to fill out, and I need to register you in our system. We won't be able to do that in time, and I can't have you disturbing the other students."

"Oh, I see." I didn't hide the disappointment in my voice.

"I can register you here, though, and you're welcome to come back. You can even sign up in advance."

"Perfect. In fact, I'll take a block of ten classes."

She cocked her head. "You don't even know if you'll like our technique."

"I'm sure it will be excellent." I strode to the desk and took my wallet from the back pocket of my sweatpants. "What do you need from me?"

"Just a credit card."

She took my American Express and handed me a clipboard with a few forms to fill out while she ran the card for a ten-class pass. I didn't bother to ask how much it cost me; I didn't care. I just took a seat on the far bench and went to work answering the questions.

I'd finished the first page when a short, barefoot woman walked into the lobby from the practice room. "Steve has the class all warmed up, and wow, that room is toasty," she said as she adjusted her ponytail. "I'm glad we decided to add hot yoga. Isn't it great that we have a full class? What did I tell you?"

"That we shouldn't worry." Natalie's attention darted my way for a half second, and that caused the woman to turn around.

"Oh!" Her eyes widened. "I didn't realize we had company."

"Don't mind me. I'm just filling out forms." I placed the clipboard back on the reception desk. "In fact, I'm done."

The woman didn't take her eyes off me. She resembled Natalie quite a bit, though her face had more unnatural points and looser skin. She also wore an expression that I'd seen plenty of times before.

Raw attraction. Desire. Blatant interest.

"Are you a new student?" she finally asked before she strolled over to my bench. "I haven't seen you here before."

Both women were pretty in their own way, but only one of them held my interest for more than a second. And that woman was behind the reception desk.

"New to this studio," I said evenly. "But not new to yoga."

"How long have you practiced?"

I glanced at Natalie, who seemed to be on the verge of laughing. "Two…ye—months. That's right. Two months."

"And you're familiar with hot yoga?"

"Y—yes."

"Well, we are happy to have you." She extended her hand and I shook it. "Just realized I haven't introduced myself. I'm Helen Mills."

"Pleased to meet you, Helen. I'm Luke Rothschild."

She stopped shaking my hand, but still held it. "Luke Rothschild? Of course."

I could almost guess the new thoughts swirling in her head. She'd heard my last name somewhere. She recognized it. And she probably thought that meant something, even though I knew it certainly didn't. People always seemed to think the name Rothschild meant more than it did.

"I'm happy to join your studio." I released Helen's hand and turned my attention back to Natalie. "And I'd love to learn more about how you think I can improve my form."

"Oh, I'm sure she has plenty of ideas," Helen purred.

"It's too bad I can't take the class today," I said.

Helen frowned. "Did you want—

"He came in too late for Steve's class," Natalie said. "He wasn't aware of our policies."

"Oh." Helen tilted her head to one side then slid her attention to the large clock hanging on the wall above the reception desk. "Well, he just began the warmup. I think we can make room for one more."

"Perfect," I said.

Helen motioned for me to follow her, and we walked to a long row of mats, yoga blocks, towels, and straps. "Do you need any of the following supplies? We have them for rental."

"Just a towel." I took the top one from a fluffy pile.

"Natalie," Helen called over my shoulder. "Add ten dollars to his account."

"Roger that," she said.

Helen smiled at me again and motioned to what looked like the locker room entrance. "Our facilities are open to all customers. If you can hurry and get changed—"

"It will only take me a moment."

I disappeared into the men's changing room, barely pausing to notice the cozy room itself, which featured long rows of wooden lockers, two benches, a sauna, and a few bathroom stalls. I threw my shoes, shirt, wallet, keys, and cell phone in a locker, then punched in a code and reemerged with my mat and towel in one hand.

"I'm ready," I said to both Helen and Natalie, who stood a few steps away from the door. I glanced down at my gym shorts. "I take it this is fine?"

Natalie's gaze floated down my chest, which was exactly what I wanted. I worked hard to maintain my physique, and I knew I had a better body than most men. My pecs had definition, and my flat stomach showed off ab muscles I'd homed in the gym and on long runs on Palm Beach's Lake Trail. She must have liked what she saw— her eyes widened, and she cleared her throat.

"Thank you for letting me join the class," I said.

"Anytime." Helen motioned behind me. "Enter right through that door."

I pivoted and walked to the door, then felt someone following behind me. I glanced over my shoulder and found Natalie, who'd grabbed the nearest mat from a group of clean ones drying on a rack.

"Since you're a new student, I'm going to make sure you don't hurt yourself," she said. "Hot yoga can be incredibly dangerous."

I laughed at her obviously made-up excuse and opened the classroom door. Inside, about twenty students lined up in front of Steve who stood in the front of the room on a mat. He gave Natalie and me a glance as we padded to the back and found two open slots near the emergency exit of the studio. I placed my mat on the floor and proceeded to mimic half-moon pose, which the other students had transitioned into as we arrived in the class. Natalie followed my lead.

"There we go," Steve said in a monotone voice that came out just over the spa-like music that added to the atmosphere of the darkened room. "Find your focus, and make sure to keep breathing. Take time to really be aware of your surroundings."

"Are you sure you know what you're doing?" Natalie whispered to me as we moved from half-moon into eagle.

"Not really," I mumbled. "But I like it that way."

Natalie

"Thank you for sharing your practice with me, class," Steve said almost an hour later as he wrapped up the session. From the front of the room, he bowed his head once then padded out of it. Within a few seconds, the students got up from their yoga mats and began to exit the space.

Luke and I, on the other hand, did not get up from our mats.

"Are you okay?" I found it hard to bite back my smile. I knew his answer before he said it.

"I'm fine," he mumbled. He lay on his back, staring at the drywall on the ceiling. Deep breaths heaved in and out of his chest.

"You're not fine. Don't lie to me." I sat up. "I've never seen anyone struggle so much with boat pose. I thought you were going to fall over on your face."

"Well, it is about a hundred ten degrees in here." He laughed and wiped his hand across his face. "And now you know my dirty secret. Despite what it looks like, I don't have great core strength."

"No, you don't." I stopped trying to hide my smile, stood from my mat, and held out a hand. "Need some help getting up?"

"I'm good." He winced and pulled himself off the mat. "I guess it's obvious that I'm not very talented at this."

"It's not where you start that matters, it's where you end up." I allowed myself to admire his chest one more time, a chest that, even glistening with sweat, still ranked as one of the top-five hottest chests I had ever seen. His defined pecs rivaled any movie star's best effort, and the small swirls of chest hair only served to entice me, inviting me to stare further.

God, this guy...

"I'll have to come back." He took his yoga mat from the floor and rolled it up. "Because now I'm determined to get what I want."

"And what's that?"

He shrugged. "A few things." He jutted his thumb toward the studio door. "Shall we catch up with the rest of the class? I need a shower."

I nodded and followed his lead. When we arrived in the lobby, a few of the other students remained, talking in small groups, cleaning their mats, and signing up for future classes. A few of the women glanced at Luke as he entered the room, and more than one gave him approving looks as he tossed his towel into the large hamper near the changing rooms and got a drink of water.

If he noticed, he didn't let on through his expression or his behavior. Instead, he told me he wanted to get changed, and he reemerged about ten minutes later with his gym bag in one hand, and a t-shirt covering his gorgeous chest. He walked up to me, and my throat went drier than a canyon in Death Valley.

"Well." I swallowed a few times, willing my saliva to return. "I guess we will see you soon for another class."

"I hope it's sooner than that." He braced his arm on the lip of the reception desk. "I mean…since I'm so bad at this. Maybe I need some private lessons."

"We offer those," Helen said from behind the desk.

I whipped my head in her direction and frowned. "We do?"

"Of course." Helen kept her expression unreadable and her voice flat. "We always want to accommodate our clients in any way that we can." She looked past me and focused on Luke. "If you would like a private lesson, we'd be happy to schedule one for you."

"I'll have to remember that." Luke rose up from the desk and took out his car keys. "In the meantime, thanks for adding me into the class today. I appreciated the challenge." He smiled at both of us and walked out the door.

Luke had barely left the studio when Helen turned to me. She had wide eyes and her bottom lip pinched between the thumb and forefinger of her right hand. "Are you kidding?"

"About what?"

"That's Luke Rothschild. *Rothschild*."

"So?"

"Don't you realize who he is?" Aunt Helen slapped her hand on the reception desk and a few pens rolled away from the notebook by the computer keyboard. "He's like European royalty. Or at least descended from it."

"So are half the people who vacation on Palm Beach. Tell me something that I don't know."

"But the Rothschilds aren't *just* royalty. They control everything. Everything. All the banking in Europe, all this land, Wall Street. They're like the guy behind the guy."

"Behind the guy, right?"

She didn't seem to catch my joke. "I can't believe he came in here. I hope he never does again."

"What? Why would you say that?"

"Because he's a Rothschild. They're shady. All kinds of hidden money and connections to Russian billionaires. And they are rich as hell."

"But you just offered him a private class."

She made a throwaway gesture with her left hand. "So?"

"So, plenty. You're being dramatic and unreasonable."

"No, I'm not. They'll do anything to maintain their power, Natalie. Anything. This is the kind of family that isn't happy unless it's at its center of power. They spend their entire lives trying to run over the little guy."

I frowned. "Well, he just bought a ten-class pass, so we'll be seeing him again."

Helen took a step backward and looked out at the parking lot like she expected him to come back at any second. "Luke Rothschild. Coming to our studio. This is unbelievable."

"Maybe." I lifted a shoulder. "And he really seems perfectly nice."

"Not to mention well endowed, right? I saw that chest, too." She cocked her head. "Oh, Natalie, you're not fooling me."

"Fooling you about what?"

"I know you well enough to know when you're interested."

"He'll come to a few classes. So what?" I distracted myself by straightening a few wayward brochures lying on top of the reception desk. "He's probably seasonal anyway, like half the people in town. It won't be a big deal if we don't make it one."

When I braced my hand on the reception desk, though, I gasped.

"What?"

"He left his credit card," I exclaimed. "He left his Amex Platinum."

"A platinum card? Who the hell leaves one of those lying around?" she asked, and crossed her arms. "Wait, don't answer that. A Rothschild, that's who."

Natalie

I could have called him to come get the credit card, but I didn't want to return it that way. I was too curious—and for once, I let that curiosity win. I would have been crazy to pass up any chance to see more about Luke Rothschild's life, and his credit card had just presented me with that opportunity.

It didn't disappoint.

Luke Rothschild lived at 546 North Ocean Boulevard, in a neighborhood of Palm Beach known for expansive and immaculate beachfront properties that came with private access to the ocean. His home was no exception—a white craftsman, clapboard mansion with a wraparound porch and a double front-door entry. It had grass that reminded me of a carpet, and a slip of private beach access across the street. A small sign on the driveway pointed to the service entrance, and I parked my car behind a blue

Ford Focus I guessed belonged to a member of the household staff.

An older man in a pair of blue overalls emerged from the side of the estate. "May I help you?" He wiped his hands on a gray towel as he walked toward me. "Is there something you need?"

"Is Lu—Mr. Rothschild home?"

It felt strange to say his name, and even stranger to call him Mr. Rothschild, but I didn't think I counted as one of his friends. I didn't know *what* I counted as. An acquaintance? A random woman?

"He's inside. May I tell him who you are?"

"Um…Natalie… Natalie Johnson."

I resisted the urge to add the words "no one" at the end of my name. Since the man didn't invite me inside, I decided to wait by the car and figure out a snappy way to reintroduce myself to Luke when I saw him again.

But I couldn't come up with anything that sounded very good in my head.

In fact, I had never been good on my feet like that. In eighth grade, I cost our team the state debate championship because I froze during the last question. In college at the University of Miami, I made a C in speech class because I flubbed the extemporaneous part of the oral exam.

And so, when Luke walked out of the back doorway, for a moment, I couldn't breathe. Couldn't speak. God, he was hot. So hot. Gorgeous. The kind of handsome that could sell a million magazines. The kind that could tempt people into purchasing watches or cologne they didn't need. And the kind of attractive that could send chills up my spine, even on a ninety-degree day.

"Nice to see you again," he called out as he moved closer to me.

"Yeah, uh… I just…" I swallowed, willing the dryness in my mouth to go away. "Good to see you, too."

"You don't sound like you're good."

"No, I am." I shook my head. "Really. Good—*great* —to see you again."

He stopped near the hood of my car. A wry grin crossed his face. "Are you stalking me, Natalie?"

My cheeks flushed with heat. *Yes, a hundred times, yes.*

When I didn't reply right away, he laughed to himself. "I guess I should expect this since I wrote my address on those forms at your studio."

"What can I say? You asked for it." I raised an eyebrow and tried to recover from being thrown off by the sheer manliness of him. "How are you feeling? Sore?"

"Nah, I think I can make it. Like I said, I'll have to start taking more classes. Maybe some private ones." Luke stopped about five feet away from me. "I have to admit, I didn't think that I would see you so soon."

"You mean you left your American Express platinum card at the studio on purpose?"

"What? I did?" His eyes twinkled.

I drew in a swift rush of air, mesmerized once again by his brooding, intense brown eyes. If bellies could also twinkle, mine did at that very moment.

I could get used to this…

"No, I didn't leave my credit card on purpose," Luke continued. "I would *never* leave behind something so important."

I smiled. "Maybe you were distracted."

"Maybe I was."

He braced his arm on my car, next to a medium-sized rust patch that never failed to remind me how much of a beater it was, and how desperate I often felt about my finances. I tried not to focus on that, though. Instead, I kept my attention on the finer details about the man before me. For example, when he grinned, his eyes brightened, and all his facial features sharpened. His arm had a light spray of freckles, and he wore a Rolex watch. He still hadn't changed out of the t-shirt and sweatpants. Up close, I noticed the faded outline of the Harvard crest in the center of the shirt.

Of course.

A man like Luke would attend a prestigious university—maybe two, and probably after completing high school at an elite private school with tuition costing more than most people made in a year. It would practically be criminal if he didn't have a pedigree with a past like that. I wondered if he'd had the grades to get in to Harvard, or if his parents made a significant donation. Not that it really mattered. It just cemented what I already knew—that Luke traveled in circles I could never get into.

He was so out of my league. But I'd always wanted things I couldn't have.

"After you left, I found the card at the desk." I took the Amex from my back pocket and examined it. It wasn't made of plastic, but something else, something thicker and sturdier than any card I'd ever carried.

"It's made of stainless steel," Luke whispered.

"It is?" I forced myself to feel steadier and more confident. "You know, I could have done some major damage on Worth Avenue with this. I bet the salesgirls at Neiman Marcus wouldn't have blinked."

"They all know me."

"I'm sure they do." I laughed at the idea of racking up charges for thousands of dollars in jewelry, designer handbags, and expensive shoes with red bottoms bearing names I couldn't pronounce. That would be fun. A total fantasy. "But I figured...you know where I work." I presented the card to him. "So, no unexpected charges."

"How kind of you."

He took the other end of the plastic, and for a second, we held it together on opposite sides, his gaze penetrating my soul. I couldn't look away, even if I'd wanted.

Part of me wanted to stare into his eyes forever.

"Drinks," he said under his breath.

"What?" I let go of my end of the card.

"A drink. Inside. Would you like to come inside for a drink?"

"Of course." The reply floated out of my mouth after barely a thought.

"Good." Luke grinned, showing off a row of perfect, pearly teeth as he slipped the American Express into his pants pocket. "I owe you at least that much for your careful protection of my credit rating."

"When you put it that way..." I clicked my teeth a few times. "How can I say no?"

Luke led me to the massive kitchen just off the side entrance to the house. That room alone had about the same square footage as my apartment, and it contained a large double oven, subzero refrigerator, center island, and a beautiful blue Mediterranean backsplash. I'd seen kitchens like this in magazines, but never up close. This one came right out of a chef's dream, and could have been photographed for any editorial spread in a glossy monthly magazine.

Wow.

"Why don't you take a seat?" Luke gestured at four black barstools that rimmed an extended countertop. I followed his orders and chose the middle one. He walked to the fridge and opened the right-hand side. "Let's see. I have red wine, soda, sparkling water, some lemonade…"

"Sparkling water is fine."

He turned around, and my stomach flipped as I noticed how the light from the kitchen window highlighted the angles of his face and sharpened his jaw. "Would you like a shot of vodka in that?"

"No, that's fine, just straight."

"You're not one of those health nuts, are you? No drinking? Juicing all the time? Lot of kale salad?" His gaze roamed my body for a brief beat, and again, a familiar deliciousness twisted in my stomach. "Since you teach yoga and all."

"Nope. Just don't like drinking on a weeknight."

"I do."

I laughed. "Noted. And just for reference, I don't like kale."

"Me either. Tastes like cardboard."

Luke took a bottle of beer from the shelf in the fridge door. "I'll drink to that." He fixed my drink, then settled down on the barstool at the other end of the countertop.

"Bottoms up." He raised his bottle of beer to me, and I raised my glass.

We both took a sip, and we didn't take our eyes off each other. In fact, for a moment, it felt like once again, he could see inside of me, all the way to the deepest and most hidden parts of my soul. I shivered at the thought— because I liked it. A lot.

I wanted him to look at me that way more. Much more.

"You're very interesting, Natalie," he said as he set down the beer.

"Come on. I'm not." I waved away his compliment. "What makes you say that?"

"Most of the women I know fall all over themselves to be around me. They think…they want something, and it's obvious. You don't seem to."

"Except for the time when I ran into your car."

He laughed. "Except for that."

I thought again about my meager efficiency apartment, the outstanding balance on my car, my student loans, my credit card debt, and the fact that most weekend nights I can barely afford one drink at the city's trendiest bars. Plus, this man had seen his share of cosmopolitan and sophisticated women in his life. I knew that without asking him. "I'm pretty boring, Luke. Nothing special. Just normal."

He laughed. "What is 'normal,' anyway?"

"Average. Simple. The ninety-nine percent. Most of the people in West Palm."

"You hardly fit the definition of the word 'average,' Natalie."

"Trust me, I do."

"Agree to disagree."

"You should see my bank balance, then." I laughed without humor and drank some sparkling water. "That's pretty…below average. Student loans, credit card payments, the whole bit. Just like almost every other millennial I know. A busted budget before I even get paid."

"Is that something you're worried about? Money?"

"A little." I shrugged and looked away, focusing for a moment on the intricate tile that made up the backsplash. Each one had a unique, scripted pattern created with blue paint. "Okay, a lot."

"Why don't you set a schedule and stick with it. You'll pay it off in no time. Simple as that."

"I wish it was that easy." I sighed, thinking about the next loan payment for the thousandth time that week. "I needed the money so that I could study marketing and business at the U. They gave me a partial scholarship, but it didn't cover all the costs. While I was there, I worked at a small insurance company in Coral Gables. They said they'd hire me full time when I graduated." I paused. "And then they'd closed."

"Just like that? That's so sad."

I glanced down at my sparkling water and cursed myself for not having taken up his offer of something stronger. "The owner died, and the whole business went into free fall. They had to lay off basically everyone. When I had trouble finding another job, my aunt offered to make me assistant manager at her studio." I shrugged. "I've been in West Palm Beach ever since."

He drank another swig of beer. "Do you like it here?"

The way he asked the question made it seem like he wanted an honest answer, not like he just longed to keep the conversation going. "No, I don't think I do. At least…not up until now."

"Hopefully, things will change soon." He paused, and his gaze met mine again. "I have to say, the whole time that you've been sitting here, I've been wondering about something."

I sucked in a rush of air. It felt like the atmosphere had changed in the kitchen. "What?"

Luke took another sip of his beer. "Are you seeing anyone?" he asked softly.

"As in *dating*?"

He nodded. "It's probably rude to ask, but I'm curious."

I shook my head. My love life was nothing more than a joke, and it had been for almost two years. My last date took place about a month before—a guy named John who worked for his family's insulation business, got drunk before we ordered appetizers, and referred to women as "babes" in regular conversation. Before that, I'd had nothing but a string of first dates that led nowhere, and I couldn't remember the last time I'd had sex.

In an age of swipe left and swipe right, dating sucked. Royally.

"I'm single," I said. "Very single."

"Good."

My eyes widened. I hadn't expected that reply. "Good?"

"Yes. Good."

There it was again—Luke had the strangest expression on his face, the kind of look that made an electric pulse rush though my body. That hadn't happened since junior year at the U, when I met Mark from Fort Myers, who drank too much cheap vodka and wanted to be an oncologist. Mark had set me off kilter too, and he was the first guy I ever thought I loved. The ten months we spent together had been some of the most intense of my life.

It hadn't ended well, though—Mark cheated. Twice.

I stayed with him because I didn't want to be alone, even though it hurt every day to keep up the relationship. It finally ended when we graduated, which seemed like the most natural time for a break. He moved to Tallahassee for medical school, and I stayed in South Florida. And since then, there hadn't been anyone else who made my heart beat faster, the back of my neck heat up, and the toes curl in my sandals.

Except Luke.

Something vibrated on top of the desk in the far end of the room. "Excuse me." Luke picked up an iPhone, read the screen, and cursed. "Just my luck."

"Is there a problem?"

"Sort of." He replaced the device. "Jennifer—a friend —was planning on accompanying me tonight to a cocktail reception that starts at seven." He sighed. "She can't make it up from Fort Lauderdale. Caught in meetings and a late condo showing for her real estate business."

"I'm sorry to hear that." I took another gulp of my drink and stood. "And speaking of which, I just looked at the time, and it's almost six. I should go so that you can get ready."

When I took a few reluctant steps toward the door, he moved in front of me and put his hand on my arm.

"Don't leave yet." His eyes searched mine, and another delicious tingle ran up and down my body. "What are you doing tonight?"

I didn't have any plans besides doing laundry, cooking ramen noodles for dinner, and watching on-demand movies. Helen had already agreed to close the studio for the night, so I wouldn't be needed there. But I also didn't want Luke Rothschild to know my life really was so boring. Not when his was clearly so interesting.

"I have a few things I need to take care of—"

"Whatever it is, can it wait? I want you to come with me." He smiled. "As my date."

Luke

"Your date?"

"Yes." I closed the space between us a little bit more. "Will you go with me?"

"But I…I don't have anything to wear to something like that."

"That's okay." I released her arm. "I have some dresses upstairs. A few might fit you."

I didn't add that the thought of her encased in a tight cocktail dress sounded exactly like what the reception needed. Palm Beach society could be so predictable some-times, but it wouldn't be with her around. She'd add some spice.

Natalie cocked her head. "Why do you have women's clothing in your house?"

I didn't have a great answer, and I knew I had to be careful about what I said next. The wrong reply would un-doubtedly open a Pandora's Box of questions about my old life with Faye Masters, and the fact that I'd spent the last few years dating every woman I could find to block out overwhelming grief I felt about her death. That plan had worked for a long time, and it had kept life without Faye from destroying my heart. But I didn't want to discuss all of that with Natalie.

Not yet.

"Long story." I motioned for her to come with me, and we walked down the center hallway, then traveled up the winding staircase to the second floor. "But I have a few, and I think they'll fit you."

I led her to one of the four guest bedrooms. The room was painted a shell pink, and decorated with a series of vintage travel advertisements for South Florida, Miami, and Key West. I opened the walk-in closet and took a few hangers off the racks. None of the dresses had been worn before; they had all just hung in the closet like silent re-minders of all that I'd lost.

"What do you think?"

Natalie took the first black garment out of my hand and gasped at the label. "Gucci?"

"That one is. The others are"—I glanced at the tags—"Prada, Fendi, and Prozena Schuler." I spread the outfits on the bed, remembering how much Faye had loved designer gowns, and shopping in general. In fact, the apparel still had the tags attached. She'd never had a chance to wear them.

I turned to Natalie and swept the thoughts of Faye from my mind. "You think one will work?"

One side of her mouth twisted upward. "I never said I'd go with you."

"You're right. You didn't." I took a step backward and waved a hand. "And you don't have to, if you don't want to." I let my gaze meet hers. "But it would be a lot better if you did."

She stared down at the clothing. "Are you sure you want me to do this?"

"Why not?"

I knew I was coming on strong, stronger than I should, but I couldn't help myself, and I didn't want to. I'd always had a weakness for interesting women, and Natalie certainly was that. I had to admit, it mostly came from the fact that she didn't act like or look like any of the women I usually encountered during Palm Beach's winter social season, or in New York's moneyed crowd. She didn't seem like she cared about who she thought I was—who everyone "thought" I was. She was also…natural. She had a petite and athletic body, small breasts, a dimple in the center of her chin, and blue eyes framed by curly, dark-blonde hair. No sign of fillers or Botox injections. No hint that she'd ever seen the inside of a plastic surgeon's office. And no caked-on makeup that betrayed years of effort underneath.

I couldn't remember the last time I'd been with a woman like this.

"Please come with me tonight," I said. "You don't know how boring these kinds of receptions can be. Once you've been to one, you've been to them all. You'll make it unique."

"You're on. I'll go." She picked up the Proenza Schuler dress and examined its collar line. "What about shoes? A purse? Jewelry?"

"All in the closet. I think the shoes are about a size eight. No one will notice if they're a little too big or too small on your feet—we won't be walking very far." I pointed at the bathroom. "Everything else is in there. Whatever you might need. A shower, anything. Hair-spray…makeup…"

"Fully stocked?"

"Of course."

"Don't you think that's a little strange?"

"No." I cleared my throat. "It's all from my past. My…fiancée—*ex*-fiancée…used this bathroom most of the time. She had good taste. Expensive taste, too."

"And once she left, you didn't get rid of it?"

"Couldn't come up with a very good reason why." I sighed. "Part of me just wanted to hang on to them, even though she never wore them."

"Why not?"

I swallowed. "She—" I cleared my throat, horrified at the sudden sting that formed there. Damn, this was harder than I'd imagined. "She, um…she died in a car accident about three months before we were supposed to get married. Faye went up to Nantucket for the weekend, and a semi-truck hit her rental car. Ran her off the road."

Natalie's eyes widened, and some of the color faded from her face.

I swallowed again; my tongue was growing thicker in my mouth with each word I spoke. "And I've been sort of drifting ever since."

"Oh, my god," she whispered, and lifted a hand toward me, but she dropped it as if she wasn't sure if I would be receptive to her comforting touch. "I-I had no idea."

"It was all over the papers…online…all of it. It was …" I studied the rows of unused, luxurious clothing and shoes, drew in the posh scent of Faye's extended absence. "It was a nightmare." When I looked at her again, I swallowed away some more of my grief. "I guess I'm surprised you didn't know about it."

The corners of her mouth softened. "I didn't."

I let out a rueful laugh. "I think you're the first person I've met who doesn't know anything about me. That's… that's refreshing."

"If you want me to Google you and find it all out, I can."

"No." I waved a hand. "You don't have to do that. Not unless you want to. Besides, you might not like what you find. The last few years of my life have been a blur. That's probably the best way to describe it."

"I can't imagine." She rubbed at her lips. Her eyes glistened, holding my gaze. "And I'm so sorry."

"It happened almost three years ago." My knees trembled. Odd. It was like Natalie brought out the emotion in me, whether I wanted it to be unleashed or not. I braced myself against the nearby dresser. "After she died, I shut people out. Drank myself to oblivion. Left New York City for good and moved down here to get away."

"That sounds horrible." Her cool hand touched my arm and she trailed her fingers in gentle swirls up my skin, causing my muscles to relax and my pulse to leap. "I've never lost anyone like that. I can't imagine."

"I drew in a deep breath. "But lately, I'm starting to live again. Things have…changed. For the better."

She nodded and rubbed on my shoulder for a moment. I got chill bumps, and all thoughts of Faye faded from my mind. Instead, I got the most outrageous urge to yank Natalie into my arms and claim her with my mouth.

But she had other ideas.

"Okay, Luke Rothschild." Natalie placed the dresses in the closet, then she glanced back at me. "You're on. You've got a deal."

SIX

Luke

About forty-five minutes later, Natalie clattered down the stairs in a pair of black, high-heeled sandals and the backless, blue-lace cocktail dress from Prada. I met her at the foot of the staircase; I also had changed into a pair of black dress pants, white dress shirt, and skinny black tie.

"You look breathtaking," I said, and I meant it. The fabric hugged the lines of her body and accentuated her lithe frame. "You *are* breathtaking."

She smiled; the red lipstick she wore made her teeth seem whiter and brighter. "You don't have to say things like that."

"Why shouldn't I? You're going to have every man's eyes on you tonight." I leaned closer and breathed in her floral perfume. "And I know what I like when I see it."

Her eyes widened, and I knew I'd knocked her off balance. *Perfect.* I had the upper hand, just the way I liked it. And, if she'd let me, I planned to keep it that way.

George, my house manager, had cleaned the BMW sedan that afternoon when I returned from the yoga class, so I decided we'd take that car to the reception. I pulled it out of the garage, then helped her in the passenger seat.

"So, you *don't* always drive the McLaren," Natalie said as I threw the car into reverse and backed down the short driveway.

"Nope. I'm not one of those assholes who always has to show off the exclusive sports car he drives." I laughed under my breath. "At least, not all of the time."

"Just on special occasions, right?"

"Exactly. The kind of special occasions that cause beautiful women to almost crash into the hood of it."

"Well, in that case, I'm glad I did."

"Me, too."

I thought for a moment about telling Natalie why I'd bought the $250 thousand McLaren—that I did it at my lowest point, in the middle of my darkest hours. After Faye died, I'd lived in a fog, alive on the outside and dead on the inside. Nothing had mattered—and it was strange.

So, I started drinking. And buying expensive toys. About a week after I relocated permanently from New York to South Florida, I walked into the McLaren dealership and wrote a check for the full amount of the car. The sales manager had been floored; even in Palm Beach, people rarely paid cash for cars costing hundreds of thousands of dollars. It had been my most extravagant impulse buy during the worst year of my life.

But I wasn't sure Natalie would understand something like that. She drove a Hyundai, worried about every penny she spent, and had student loans to pay. I'd probably sound like a jerkoff to her.

"We don't have to stay long at this reception," I said instead. "It all depends on you."

The event took place in the back room of Nicolao's, a restaurant and bar about a five-minute drive from my place. We could have walked there, but it didn't work that way in Palm Beach. People wanted to make an entrance, and everything about receptions like this one had to be orchestrated. Nothing could be out of place. True, Palm Beachers wanted their cars, money, access, and designer clothing to be seen, especially by people they didn't know. It had always been that way, and it would never change.

I'd been playing this game on and off for five years; I knew it well. Some might even say I'd mastered it.

I parked the BMW in an open parking spot across from the restaurant, helped Natalie out of the car, and escorted her across the street. The restaurant sat at the end of a long row of shops and storefronts. I nodded at a few of the immaculately dressed patrons eating dinner on the semi-covered patio, and waved at a few others.

When we reached the hostess stand, my palm grazed the small of Natalie's muscular back. She didn't pull away. I liked that; I wanted more of it.

And I planned to get it.

Soon.

"Right this way, Mr. Rothschild."

The hostess pivoted on a sky-high, pink heel and led us to the back of the building: a pavilion strewn with a few tables, couches covered in outlandish, printed pillows, a small private bar, a few indoor plants, and strands of white lights overhead. About two dozen people already mingled in the center of the room, and I recognized many of them.

Even more reacted to our entrance as if they knew me—the kind of familiarity that had always come from having the Rothschild last name.

"Showtime," I muttered. Natalie's laughter rippled through my hand just before I removed it from her shapely back.

"Luke," called Maryanne Plunkett, one of Palm Beach's resident socialites, "so wonderful to see you tonight." She glided toward the two of us and I leaned down to kiss both of her tight cheeks, ones that didn't match her seventy-five years of age. Maryanne had very good doctors, of course, and like many women in Palm Beach, she paid for it. Or rather, *her husband* paid for it. "Oh, I'm so happy you're here."

"Thank you for having us."

She placed her manicured fingers on my arm, and I smelled a familiar whiff of Shalimar perfume. The scent reminded me of my own grandmother, a straight-laced woman who'd started the family's Palm Beach tradition by insisting on a vacation on the island at least once a year. "We couldn't have this event without you. You know that."

"Don't be silly."

"I'm not." Maryanne grinned before she glanced at Natalie. "And who's this?"

"May I present Miss Natalie Johnson?" I turned to my date, who extended her own hand.

"Pleased to meet you," Natalie said as she greeted Maryanne. "What a wonderful evening for a party."

"Of course, darling." Maryanne dropped Natalie's hand and visibly sized her up. "And are you down for the season?"

Natalie suppressed a grin. "I… No, ma'am, I live here year-round."

"On the island? I'm surprised we've never met."

I cleared my throat, knowing where this conversation would head. Natalie had about ten seconds to make an impression with Maryanne, and she'd need my help to do it. "Natalie helps run a successful yoga studio in West Palm. Has quite a following, actually."

"Yoga? Oh, really?" Maryanne's eyes brightened. "I've been meaning to get back into that. My doctor says it will be good for my overall health. Do you have Pilates, as well? I *love* Pilates."

"Not yet, but we'll be adding that soon."

Maryanne cocked her head. "A shame you're over the bridge, though. I simply hate venturing over there."

"You should try it sometime." I put my hand on Natalie's back once more and felt her lean into it. "You might like what you find. I sure did."

Natalie chuckled to herself. "Luke's a new student at our studio." She jerked her head in my direction. "He's relearning…downward dog."

"That I am," I said, no longer caring about Maryanne Plunkett and her too-tight facelift. "And I'm lucky to have such an excellent teacher."

As if on cue, a server in a white dress shirt breezed by the three of us with a tray of champagne flutes. I grabbed two and handed them to the ladies before taking one for myself. "To another fantastic evening in paradise," I said. "Cheers."

"Cheers," they repeated, before taking long sips. When they finished, we had the out we needed. Maryanne's attention turned to someone who had arrived after us, and she excused herself, so she could greet them, as well.

I leaned down and put my mouth near Natalie's earlobe. "Good work. You passed the first test."

"Test? I wasn't aware this was an exam."

"In Palm Beach, everything always is."

"Meaning?"

"The people at a party like this always want anyone they meet to seem interesting, like decorative potted plants. They insist that newcomers 'enhance' the flow." I let my attention drop to the swell of breasts I saw peeking out from the neckline of Natalie's cocktail dress. "I'd say you did that very well." I lifted my gaze again and tightened my arm around her waist. "So, congratulations."

Man, I was coming on thick...

"Thank you," she said, but I still saw her hesitate.

"Don't believe it?" I swallowed the rest of the champagne and placed the empty glass on the nearby bar. "Maryanne Plunkett is one of those ladies you'll see everywhere when—if—you start spending time over here. If she likes you, you're in," I said in a lowered voice.

"In where?"

"All of the parties. The private receptions. Society."

"And you go along with that?"

"Along with what?"

"This? All this tete-a-tete? That kind of decorum?"

"Of course," I said. "It's just how things work. It's tradition. And if you don't know the rules, you can't win."

"You like to win, don't you?"

"When I can." I cocked my head. "And especially when it's something that I want."

Natalie

W e lived in different worlds. No question about it. No matter what, that would never change. But I also found his world fascinating.

Luke Rothschild had more money than anyone I'd ever met, and just the way people looked at him that night told me that he also had a lot of power, the kind that didn't come overnight. All the partygoers seemed to defer to him, and more than one appeared focused on making sure he acknowledged them over the passing around of plates full of canapés, smoked salmon, and miniature quiches. Systematically, he worked the room, too, and we posed more than once for photographers who told me they worked for various society publications.

I got the feeling that Luke Rothschild liked the life he led and the status he held. No, not just that. He was *comfortable* with it.

"Did you have a good time?" Luke asked as he drove us back to his house.

"I did. Delicious smoked salmon."

"Nicolao's does that very well. You should try their guacamole, too. Excellent."

I chuckled. "You have a thing for guacamole, don't you?"

"A thing?"

"It's the second time you've brought up guacamole to me. You also said you liked the one they have at Rocco's Tacos."

Luke blinked at me. "I did?"

I nodded.

"Well, I'm—what can I say? I like it." He snapped his fingers. "Consider me a guacamole connoisseur."

"I'll have to remember that."

My attention wandered back to the car window and I watched the city streets pass. My thoughts rewound to the party we'd just attended. When was I ever going to step foot in a restaurant like that again? Best guess—never. That place had white tablecloths and exotic champagne stocked at the bar. I probably couldn't afford a glass of wine there, let alone dinner.

But it had been fun to be on Luke's arm. More than fun. Intoxicating.

Luke maneuvered the BMW into the driveway and stopped the car in front of the garage. "I had a good time with you tonight. Thank you for being my last-minute date."

"You're welcome. Any time."

And, of course, I meant that. Luke lived a life that would be easy to fall in love with, if I let myself. He owned a beautiful beach house, a car that cost several hundred thousand dollars, and he spent his free time drinking expensive liquor with people who worried about things like where to vacation for Christmas. My meager reality didn't resemble his at all.

Remember that, remember that, remember that...

I hooked my fingers around the passenger door handle. "I guess I better get going. What should I do with the outfit? Have it cleaned?"

His gaze roamed over my body, spending a little extra time on the swell of my small breasts. "Keep it."

"Can I pay you for it?"

He shook his head.

"I couldn't—"

"You should. It's yours. I don't have any use for it. And it looks great on you."

"But...you don't have to give me something like this. It's too nice of you."

"Just thank me," he whispered.

I swallowed. "Thank you."

We fell silent. His stare met mine again, and I sucked in a sharp breath. Was he going to kiss me? Did I want him to?

What was I doing here?

"Good night, Natalie," he said instead.

My heart sank a little. The night was over. Time to get back to my real life. The fantasy had ended.

"Good night."

I got out of the car and walked over to my own vehicle. As I unlocked it with my key fob, I heard him climb from the BMW and trot over to me.

"Wait," he said as his hand caught my shoulder. I whirled around, and his gaze searched my face once more.

"What?"

Please kiss me…

"You left your clothes inside."

I blanched. "I did?"

"Let me go get them." He spun and jogged into the house, then returned a few minutes later with a small black tote bag. "Here you are. Wouldn't want you to miss these."

"Thank you." I took the bag and our gazes locked. I sucked in a deep breath and held it inside my chest. The way he looked at me—I longed for him to look at me like that for the rest of my life.

"I want to see you again." He brushed a strand of hair off my cheek and tucked it behind my ear. His gaze followed his own movements. A warm tremor moved from my ear, down my neck, and into my lower belly. He shifted his eyes up and locked his gaze with mine. "Tomorrow night. Dinner. Would you like that?"

"Yes," I whispered, mesmerized by the deepness of his voice. "Absolutely."

His mouth twisted into a half-smile. "Good. What's your phone number?"

SEVEN

Natalie

"Snap out of it," Helen said the next morning as she shuffled past the reception desk with a basket full of used towels. She stopped at the edge of the counter and regarded me over a small mountain of fresh towels piled into the laundry basket. "You're a trillion miles away today."

She was right. I'd been thinking about Luke on and off ever since I left his house. In fact, I'd hardly slept because every time I closed my eyes, I saw the way he looked: chiseled jaw, natural tan, soulful eyes... I blinked a few times and shook my head. I knew better than to tell Helen any of this. She wouldn't get it.

"Sorry," I said. "Just thinking about something."

"Well, whatever it is, you're distracted, and it's written all over your face."

"I know." I shook the mouse by the computer to wake it. "But it's nothing. I promise."

Nothing and everything at the same time…

Helen shifted the basket and balanced it between her hip and the counter. "I meant to ask you earlier—do you remember Josh's friend? Keith?"

"Yes." I tried to keep a straight face and the dread out of my voice as I answered her. "What about him?"

"Well, he really wants to meet you. So, I'm thinking, maybe next week the four of us can go out. Sturkey's?"

Josh, Helen's *much* younger boyfriend, tended bar at Sturkey's three nights a week to earn some extra money. During the day, he worked as a spinning instructor and personal trainer at the Atlantic Tide Resort, a place he said should have paid him twice what he made. He always claimed he worked there reluctantly, but he hadn't tried to get a new job, either. I suspected he liked it more than he wanted to admit.

Josh also had biceps larger than my thigh, and when that man "had to eat," he could pack away three hamburgers in one meal. He talked about bodybuilding and not much else. That type. I could only imagine what Keith would be like.

"That'd be great," I lied. "Set it up."

"You sound thrilled."

My phone vibrated, signaling I had a text message. I resisted the urge to look at it. "I am."

Helen cocked her head. "Let me guess. You're still thinking about Luke Rothschild, aren't you?"

I tried to keep my expression unreadable. My aunt had a big mouth, and once she had a plan, she dug in. There would be no changing her mind. Plus, I didn't feel like I could tell her much about my love life. She might have been my aunt, but she was also my boss. Didn't want to make things more complicated.

"Luke's a nice guy," I said. "And I hope he comes in here soon to take another class."

Sounded good. Non-committal. After all, what was I to Luke, anyway? We'd gone to a reception, and we had plans that night, but so what? It could mean anything— especially for a guy like him. I wouldn't have been surprised to hear that he had dozens of women at his disposal.

"Let's do something with Keith next week, just like you said," I added.

"Perfect." Helen slapped her free hand on the countertop. "I'll let him know."

She crossed to the large hamper on the far end of the room, the one closest to the women's changing room, and proceeded to add some of the towels to her basket. I let out a small sigh. Helen really wanted to make this "thing" between me and Keith happen, and she'd been trying for months to force it. She'd spent an unusual amount of time talking Keith up, telling me how nice he was, and a few times she'd shown me various photos from his Instagram and Snapchat accounts.

But he wasn't my type. However, it would be much easier to tell her that I didn't want to date Keith *after* I'd met him. Less conflict that way—which I avoided with Helen whenever I could.

"Oh, I meant to tell you something." She closed the hamper and turned around to face me. Her expression changed, and she arched one eyebrow. She wanted me to listen very carefully to what she had to say next. After a breath, Aunt Helen said, "I looked up Luke Rothschild on my phone last night."

"And?"

"His life is complicated at best. Did you hear about the dead fiancée? Totally strange. And sad."

"Oh?" I made sure to raise my voice and widen my eyes, so I sounded more believable and more stunned. I had no plans to tell her about my impromptu turn as Luke's date, or about the designer dress I had stashed away in the back of my closet. "I hadn't heard about that."

"She died about three years ago in a terrible car accident. And since then, he's been just...drifting."

"Really?" Again, I took care to keep my voice nonchalant. "That's sad."

"Absolutely. And just like I suspected—his dad is *Barrett Rothschild*." She said this as if the name Barrett should trigger a negative reaction from me. I didn't give her one. "Barrett Rothschild was the one who funded that huge hedge fund, Harvest Capital. And he spent the whole Great Recession making a killing buying foreclosed homes and businesses in New York. Including ones owned by senior citizens."

"You're kidding?"

"Would I joke about something like that?" Helen held her mouth agape and rushed a few steps toward me. "He profited off people's pain, Natalie. He made money off their misfortune—almost $500 million in three years. But, I guess I shouldn't be that surprised. He's a rich guy. You know how *those* people are."

I had only one way to respond to my aunt's comments, and I knew it. "Totally."

For the last eighteen months or so, I'd watched Helen become more and more socially active. Everything she talked about these days circled back to community involvement, social justice, and an "us versus them" mentality. "We can't afford to stay on the sidelines," she often said. "There's too much at stake." I didn't disagree with her, but I also didn't see everything from behind the same lens.

But anytime I'd tried to bring this up with her, my aunt had either interrupted me, or walked away.

"That's a lot of money," I added. "A whole lot."

And it was—I couldn't think of how much money $500 million would really be. Did they have bank accounts for that kind of figure? Where did that money go? Was it real, or tied up in investments? Could you access that kind of cash all at once? Didn't banks have account balance caps?

"Also, get this…" Helen gave me a knowing look. "*Page Six* recently reported that Barrett wants to give control of the family's New York commercial real estate business to his oldest son, Luke, but that he won't do it until Luke gets married. He even threatened to disinherit him if he turns thirty-five and isn't engaged to someone."

"Really? *Engaged?*" I quickly coughed a few times and looked away. "I'm sorry. I just didn't expect you to say that."

"Of course, that means someone 'acceptable.' Someone blue-blooded. You know how rich people think. Only the best for them."

"Oh, yes, you're right," I said, but the words tasted hallow and meaningless in my mouth.

"Then there's that whole thing with Faye Masters. So sad." Helen clicked her tongue against her teeth. "The state police said the driver of the semi-truck fell asleep at the wheel."

"And they were set to get married just a few months later."

Helen's eyes widened.

"I mean…that's what I assume—that the wedding wasn't far away?" I glanced back at my aunt and hoped my expression would help her buy my next lie. "Since you said she was his fiancée."

"Hmm," she said after a moment. "Regardless, the people in the one percent are so weird. They don't live normal lives."

"You have to admit, though, he's hot. And he seems …*seemed* like a really nice guy." It was about as close as I wanted to get to confessing how much I'd been thinking about Luke in the last week.

Which had been a lot.

"He's good looking in a too-rich-for-his-own-good kind of way. I *will* give him that." Helen moved down the hall to the small linen closet where we stored the studio washing machine and dryer.

I watched her until I knew for sure she wasn't paying attention to me. Then I flipped over the phone.

Luke: *Hey there. Pick you up at 8?*

Interesting.

I glanced down the hall at Helen. The mass of towels still distracted her.

Me: Perfect. See you then. I'm at 4530 Flager Dr. Apartment 16.

Luke

Natalie lived in a large apartment complex that rimmed a central, in-ground pool, the kind of place developers built in less than six months, marketed to twentysomethings, and overcharged for on the rent. I parked the car in front of the second unit of eight apartments and jogged up the stairs to hers. She cracked open the door a moment after I rapped on it.

"I'd invite you in," she said as she stepped out in the breezeway and closed the entryway to her apartment, "but it's embarrassing."

"No, it's not."

"My apartment is tiny."

"So?"

She locked the deadbolt and dropped her key in her black tote bag. "Have you ever lived in an apartment, Luke?"

"Of course. In Manhattan."

"Park Avenue doesn't count." She began to walk down the stairwell, and I followed her. She wore a black skirt, gold flat sandals, a lightweight, white sweater, and a gold necklace. She stayed a few steps ahead of me, and I admired her ass.

Nice, round, and just the right amount of perky.

"I never lived on Park Avenue," I said.

"Well, the entire Upper East Side doesn't count. Neither does Tribeca, or Soho…"

"How about Greenwich Village?" I asked as we reached the main sidewalk that linked the units and parking lot together. "I lived there for about two years after college."

She shook her head.

"Brooklyn? My cousin had a place there a few years ago. A brownstone with a few units. One of those rehabbed buildings in a gentrified neighborhood full of hipster assholes with long beards and ten-dollar espresso habits."

"Nice description." She laughed, and we kept on walking. "But nope. Still doesn't count."

"I don't care where you live. It doesn't matter to me. I want to get to know you." I unlocked the car with my key fob and opened the passenger door. "I mean that."

"I keep asking myself why." She got in the car, looked up at me, and held my gaze with probing, brilliant pools of green. "Doesn't make sense."

"Not everything in life must," I replied as I shut the door.

We had a reservation at Renato's, a restaurant tucked just off Worth Avenue. Just like Nicolato's, people liked to be "seen" at this bistro, and when we arrived, the host led us to a quiet table overlooking the sidewalk and Worth Avenue's luxury shops. I settled into a seat across from

Natalie and asked for a bottle of chardonnay from the extensive list.

"I take it you've eaten here before." She opened the leather-encased menu and scanned it.

"Many times."

"And what's good?"

I made a few suggestions, and the waiter returned with the bottle of wine. He poured us two glasses, and we settled on two entrees, the linguini and the rigatoni. Soon, we found ourselves alone again.

"It's a beautiful night," I said, making a sad attempt at small talk.

"It is." She regarded the rest of the diners on the patio. "This place is packed."

"Always during the winter, even on a Tuesday night."

"I never make my way over here, so I wouldn't know."

"First time for everything." I raised my wine glass. "Cheers to that."

She lifted hers, too. "Cheers."

We both sipped our wine, but when Natalie put down her glass, she furrowed her brow, and her gaze didn't meet mine anymore.

"What's on your mind?"

"Nothing." She looked away, over the railing and up the sidewalk.

I shifted in my seat. "Come on. You don't mean that."

She exhaled. "Okay. I've just been...thinking about something." She broke off for a moment, and I sipped my wine, waiting. "What's going on with you and your father?"

"Oh, I see. Someone's been Googling, huh?"

"No." She shook her head with vehemence, causing her hair to tumble over her shoulder. Then she acted as if I'd accused her of a crime. "No, *I* haven't. Helen did."

I nodded as things became clearer to me. "And of course, a few articles from the New York media came up right away, among other things."

I drank some more chardonnay and reminded myself to remain calm, even though the mention of what the New York City tabloids had written annoyed me. They often got it wrong, but in this case, they'd gotten most of it right, and that felt worse. Dirty laundry that didn't need airing.

"My father is an...*interesting* man, and so is our family."

"I can't say that I'm surprised."

"And yes, what you've read is mostly true. My father wants to hand over control of his real estate empire to me as his oldest son, but he won't do it until I find 'the one'— if she lives up to what he wants. And if I reach thirty-five before finding her, he won't give me any of it. Not one penny."

She grimaced. "That seems extreme."

"I don't disagree with you." I waved a hand. "He'll be forced to put his life's work in a trust for my half-brother Marcus, who is fourteen, and a freshman at Phillips Exeter Academy."

"And he doesn't want to do that because...?"

"My father is seventy. He wants to retire as soon as possible, and he's thinking about his...legacy. Leaving the company to Marcus means he can't retire until Marcus finishes college, maybe eight years or so from now."

Simple and complex all at the same time. I knew my place in the world, but ever since Faye's death, I'd had trouble accepting it. It kept feeling like I was living a life that wasn't mine.

And I didn't like that.

Most people would have been content inheriting their father's company and continuing an expected legacy, but for the last few years, it hadn't been a comfortable path for me. I knew I had the talent to handle my father's empire; however, allowing my life to become part of his monarchy had always felt hollow and unfulfilling.

But maybe it was time for a change.

Natalie gulped. "What you are saying sounds complicated."

"It is, in a way. But in other ways, I guess, it's simple."

She raised her glass to her lips. "So, when is your thirty-fifth birthday?"

"Next month." I laughed at the tremendous absurdity of it all, and just as she was taking a sip of her drink, I blurted, "I've always been good at taking things to the wire."

She tried to swallow, but the wine came back up and she began to choke.

"Are you okay?" I scooted my chair back, stood then sat again. "Can you breathe?"

Still coughing, she held up a hand and didn't answer.

"Natalie, what can I do to help you?"

"No, I'm..." She cleared her throat a few times, waved her hand in front of her face, and gulped. "Whew."

"Are you sure you're all right?" I decided I knew the answer to my own question. "No, I don't think you are." I signaled to the waiter standing at a nearby table. "Can we get some more water, please?" The waiter nodded and scurried away to find some while Natalie wheezed a few more times. "Try to take a few bigger breaths."

Her eyes were watery, her voice scratchy. "I-I'm…fine. I mean it, I think I'll be fine." She cleared her throat one last time. "I-I just didn't expect that answer."

"Yes, I know. Next month. It's close."

The waiter I'd signaled arrived at the table with a fresh glass of water, then asked Natalie if she needed anything else. When he left us alone again, we sat in silence for a few moments.

"So, you're in danger of losing your easiest opportunity to become a billionaire in less than thirty days?" she finally said.

"Something like that. I'd be lying if I said it wasn't on my mind a lot recently. But I also don't like to force things." I paused. "Especially not relationships."

The server assigned to our table arrived with our two entrees, announced our meals, and put the plates in front of us. After remarking about how delicious they looked, we both took our first few bites.

"Wow," she said after her fourth one. "This truly is wonderful."

"This restaurant has been here for as long as I can remember. It's one of my favorites for a reason." We ate in silence for several moments before I decided to continue the conversation. "I said earlier that I don't like to force things."

Natalie placed her fork on the plate, chewed, swallowed, and dabbed at her moist lips with her napkin. "Yes?"

"I'll admit—I want that money. It's a lot, and a part of me wants to claim it. I'd just about given up on ever getting it before I met you. Or rather, before you ran into my McLaren."

Her cheeks flushed.

"Since then, I've been thinking…" I took a deep breath. "What if I gave you a million dollars to spend the next month with me, and help me convince my father that I'd found the one?"

EIGHT

Natalie

I pulled in a lungful of air, and it caught in my throat. "Excuse me?"

Joking. He *had* to be joking. Right? This wasn't serious. It didn't make sense. He didn't mean it.

Did he?

"I'm not sure I understand what you're saying." Confusion and shock both coursed through my body in a hot flash. What was this?

Luke rubbed his hand across his chin. "It's a lot to ask, but we have chemistry. *A lot* of chemistry. You've got to admit it."

"Yes, but—"

"I've been thinking, and I figure…a million dollars is enough money to make a difference to you."

I tried to reply, but I couldn't think of anything to say. Instead, I pushed myself against the back of my chair and tried to sort through what sounded to me like nonsense.

"I felt something when I first saw you, in those seconds after you almost hit my car," Luke said. "Something different. Something real." He offered me another glass of wine, which I refused, and then he poured himself a generous second glass. "You're more interesting than the other women I know. And you're...sexy in your own way."

"Sexy? If you mean that—"

He raised a hand. "That's not the right way to put it. Forgive me. I just... I like you. I want to get to know you. And it just so happens there's money to be made in all of this."

"A million dollars." Saying the number felt strange. "A *million* dollars?"

"For you, yes. As soon as my father gives me control of the company. When it's airtight, and the ink is dry."

I stared at him. "You've thought this through, haven't you?"

He shrugged.

"What do you think I am?"

"It's one month of your life, Natalie. Maybe six weeks. This isn't forever."

I ate another bite of pasta, which now tasted like year-old ramen noodles.

"My father is a mercurial man," Luke said. "He wants things done his way."

"What does *that* mean?"

"Last night was a good start. Our photo wound up in the *Palm Beach Daily News* this afternoon, and I emailed my father the link to the website. He likes to keep track of news items like that. He's...particular. It's all about Rothschild brand to him."

"And what? We date for the next six weeks, he gives you control of the company, and we go our separate ways?"

Luke made a move like he wanted to reach across the table and take my hand, but then he hesitated. "We can make this a legal contract if you want. Or you can just trust me." He paused. "I'm talking about a million dollars, Natalie, and I'm not even requiring you to have sex with me."

The word "sex" hung in the air for a second after he said it.

We stared at each other, and my toes curled in my shoes. No, he wasn't requiring that I sleep with him, but I wanted to. I knew that much. I also knew I'd do it for far less than a million dollars. I'd do it for nothing.

"What is your family's company worth?" I finally managed. "A couple of million?"

"You really don't know, do you?" Luke grinned. "And that's what I like about you." He lowered his voice, making it deeper and silkier. "Rothschild International Acquisitions has properties and holdings worth about seven billion."

I gasped. "That much? Seven b-billion?"

"It's a large number, and it fluctuates according to the market." He shifted his weight in the chair. "But we're never worth less than four billion in liquid assets. It is separate from what I've made on my own…which isn't much. And the minimal trust fund that my father gave me when I reached twenty-five is almost gone, so you can see why I need—no, why I want—that money. It's *my* rightful half of the company—which I receive *only* if I'm engaged before I turn thirty-five." He paused. "And that means that your acceptance of my modest offer would be… meaning-ful."

I could only imagine what that number would end up being. Even *one* billion dollars felt astronomical, like something I couldn't comprehend, to say nothing of what four would mean.

Still, I needed to keep my cool. Remain calm. Act natural.

I swallowed and forced my face to stay almost ex-pressionless. "What you're saying is, one million dollars is chump change. 'Modest' chump change. Hardly anything. A small price to pay for gaining control of that kind of money."

"I would never say that." His gaze roamed my body and lingered on the neckline of my shirt, causing my nip-ples to involuntarily tighten. "What I'm really saying is, I'd like you to join me." He moved his attention back to my eyes. "What do you think?"

Luke

"You don't have to answer that right away," I said after a pause that lasted an eternity. "I wouldn't ask that of you. This is a big deci-sion, and those shouldn't be made in haste."

I knew I was coming on strong again, and I wondered if I'd gone too far, if I'd just suggested something preposterous. It hadn't sounded so strange in my head; I'd first had the idea as I ended my golf game with Aaron, and it had only grown the more I'd spent with Natalie. By the time I made the offer over expensive pasta, it seemed like a natural, reasonable thing to do. Why not mix a little business with pleasure? People did that all the time.

But maybe I'd been wrong.

"What's the catch?" Natalie finally asked. "There *has* to be a catch."

"Just my company, if you can stand me."

"I'm not…"

I gestured with a hand. "What you see is what you get. I'm a man of my—"

"Luke Rothschild! I thought I saw you there!" Gerald Levy walked the few final steps to our table and clapped me on the shoulder. I'd been so engrossed in my conversation with Natalie that I hadn't noticed him. "Wonderful to see you tonight."

"Gerald, great to see you, as well." I stood from the table and buttoned my navy sport coat. "I didn't realize you were in town."

"Just for a long weekend. Must head back to the city for a few meetings on Monday. We're taking SnapDate public on Tuesday, so it's going to be hectic."

"SnapDate?" Natalie rose from her chair, and I cursed myself for not having better manners. "The app?"

"I'm sorry," I told her. "Let me introduce you all. Natalie Johnson, this is Gerald Levy. Gerald, please meet Miss Natalie Johnson."

The two shook hands.

"Sounds like you have a busy week," I said.

Gerald nodded and ran a hand through his silver hair. "Hopefully my last IPO as a venture capitalist. I'm getting too old for this kind of game." He winked at Natalie. "Will I see you at your father's party on Wednesday night?"

"Of course," I said. "Wouldn't miss it."

"Excellent." He glanced over his shoulder. "My wife is here, and she doesn't like to be kept waiting. I'll leave you two to your meal, and I'll see you in New York on Wednesday."

The three of us said goodbye, and once Gerald had left us, we sat at our table once more. Natalie's eyebrows knitted together. "New York?"

"The company is commemorating the thirtieth anniversary of Rothschild Center, my father's first major building in Manhattan." Natalie's eyes widened, and I decided to ignore this reaction by readjusting my napkin. "He's very proud of it."

"I didn't realize you all owned Rothschild Center."

"Among other things."

"I probably should have assumed, but I'd never thought about it." She drank some more wine. "And that man is taking SnapDate public?"

"He's one of the initial investors. You sound familiar with it."

She shrugged one shoulder. "Everyone uses SnapDate these days."

"That's right. *Fast Company* did say it was responsible for the death of modern romance. I think *Cosmopolitan* said the same."

She laughed. "I wouldn't know."

I studied her for a moment, considering my options. "How about this—I'm leaving for New York on Wednesday morning. If you want to… How about you join me? Can you get away from the yoga studio for one night, even if it's late notice?"

She studied me for a long moment before she shook her head. "No. I can't."

"What?"

"I've been thinking about your offer and…it's not right for me. I can't do this."

"But—"

Natalie pushed her chair back from the table. "I'm not for sale. I'm not a prostitute."

What? Where was this coming from?

I frowned. "I never said you were one. I know that you're not. I could never think that about you."

"It's no secret that I need the money. I do. I could use a break like this. But I'm…" She stood. "Goodnight, Luke."

"Wait, what?" I stood, too, my voice rising with each word I spoke. A woman sitting at the next table stared at us in between sips of red wine. I ignored her, even though she looked familiar. All I cared about in that moment was Natalie. "I didn't mean it the way that it sounded."

"Yes, you did." Natalie glanced at the woman sitting at the nearby table and lowered her voice. "You know what? We don't live in the same world, Luke. It's so obvious. I've never seen anything clearer." She squared her shoulders. "Have a good night."

88

Natalie spun and pushed her way through the crowded restaurant. I stared at her in disbelief for a few seconds, but it could have been an eternity.

Shit, I've done it again. Just like I always did.

I'd ruined a good thing before it even started. No wonder I'd kept my love life simple and straightforward in the wake of Faye's death. Easier to focus on the sex and leave the emotions out of it.

I didn't do complicated very well, and I'd just gotten a hell of a reminder.

"Natalie, wait," I called after her. If she heard me, she didn't respond.

"My god," muttered the woman at the adjacent table.

I gave her the briefest glance, found my wallet in my back pocket, left $200 on the table, and rushed out of the restaurant. "Wait," I said again when I reached the street. "Natalie, come on!" I sprinted down the sidewalk and put a hand on her shoulder.

She whirled around. "What?"

"Please. Give me another shot." I panted a few times. "I didn't mean to come across that way."

She folded her arms. "I think you did."

"I just…it was an idea that I had the other day. I wanted to see what you thought."

"Now you know."

"You have to understand—for the last few years, everything in my life has been transactional." I closed the space between us. "That's how I'm used to dealing with things. It's been that way for so long that I've forgotten how to do it any other way. And I guess…" I cleared my throat. "Money is freedom, right? It buys freedom. And that's power."

She shook her head and began walking down the street. I followed her, and neither of us spoke for several blocks.

"I know I screwed up," I finally said. "I did."

"It's not just that." She sighed. "You're used to having—just *buying*—everything you want, aren't you? You don't know another way."

"Maybe, but what's wrong with that?"

"Plenty." She gave me a sideways glance. "Why are you hanging around me, Luke? Have you asked yourself that?"

"I have." I cleared my throat. "And the answer is that you're not like the other women I know. You don't take things for granted. Like the other night, when you didn't want to take that dress." I hoped my explanation for this crazy plan would disarm her. "I like that kind of thing about you. You're not interested in me just because I'm 'Luke Rothschild,'—whatever that means."

"It sounds like it means something to *a lot* of people."

I leaned closer to her. "I agree. But you're not one of them."

She gestured at the luxury stores that lined Worth Avenue and the row of BMWs, Infinities, and sports cars in the parking spots on both sides of the street. "This world isn't my world."

"Doesn't mean it can't be."

Natalie regarded me for a moment. "I don't see how this could work."

"I do."

We reached the end of Worth Avenue, and the large clock tower in front of the beach loomed ahead of us. Natalie raised her hand and signaled to the passing vehicles that she wanted to cross the street. When we reached the tower, she fished her phone out of her purse.

"What are you doing?"

"Calling for a ride." She unlocked her phone.

"I'll take you home."

"No, you won't." She focused on the taxi-service app for a few seconds. "Okay…two minutes or less. They are right around the corner." She locked her phone, put it back in her bag, and crossed her arms. "It's better this way, Luke. We have nothing in common. You have everything. I am…we don't fit."

"I think we could."

"Best of luck in New York." One side of her mouth twisted into a half-smile. "And thanks for dinner."

"Anytime."

A Nissan Sentra pulled up to the curb. The driver rolled down the passenger window. "Are you Natalie?"

"That's me," she told him, then gave me one more look. "Goodbye, Luke Rothschild."

"Goodbye, Natalie Johnson."

With a small wave, she got into the car and left the island.

NINE

Natalie

We had nothing in common. *Nothing.*

I knew that. We lived less than fifteen minutes away from each other, but our lives didn't connect at all. Plus, I was insulted.

"Forty-five thirty Flagler," I told the driver after I closed the car door. I knew the app would tell him the destination, but I didn't care. I just wanted to say something and set the driver on his way. As the car pulled away from the curb, I forced myself to not look back. I couldn't take one more glance at this man, a person who had tipped my world off its axis in just a few short days.

When I arrived at my apartment, I stripped off my skirt and sweater, then threw them in the hamper in the corner of my bedroom. I stopped at my open closet door and found the designer dress he'd given me, hanging on the rod next to the few formal clothes that I owned. I fingered the silky material and thought about the night he'd given it to me, the first time it had really come into focus, how expensive and interesting Luke Rothschild's life was. Even then, he'd been buying my time.

Right? I'd made a good decision, right? Saying no to him made sense, right?

If I wanted to be honest with myself, I couldn't be sure.

A Few Days Later

"What's on your mind, son?" My father adjusted his bowtie in the hall mirror just outside the room where I stayed whenever I visited him in New York. "You've been quiet ever since you got here."

"Just thinking about a few things," I said as I joined him in the hallway. "Business."

He braced his hand on the wall. "You? Business? Hardly. What you do in Palm Beach isn't business. It's playtime."

I offered a dry laugh. "Like you would know."

"I do." He eyed me. "You know how I feel about the trajectory of your life. The sooner you get in line, the better."

"And you've said that a thousand times."

"Doesn't change the fact that it's the truth."

"I've had a rough few years, Dad." I sighed. "You know that."

"I do." He clapped a hand on my shoulder. "And I sympathize, I promise. I know you took Faye's death hard. That you were shattered. We all were, and it was a tragedy. We all mourned her. We still do."

I searched his eyes for something that resembled genuine concern and empathy. When I wasn't sure I found it, I didn't give him a reply.

"I know your time in Palm Beach has been therapeutic. You've spent time working on yourself and donated to causes that mean a lot to you. I know that you've needed this. It's helped you process what happened with her death." He tightened his hand. "But…you can't keep wallowing in it, and your life in Florida only keeps you doing that."

"I happen to *like* my life in Florida."

Dad set his mouth into a hard line. "I have plans for this company. Plans for you."

"I know. And I think—"

"You haven't wanted to be a Rothschild for years, have you son? You'd walk away from this if you could, wouldn't you?"

"No, that's where you're wrong." I swallowed, willing some saliva to return to my mouth, which suddenly felt very dry. "I want to rejoin the company, and take my place at your side, but I want to do it on my terms. How it makes sense for me. I won't do it according to your plan." Our gazes locked. "That's what you've never understood, Dad. You don't control me. I'm not one of your assets."

"Whatever you say, son." He pulled his hand off my shoulder, a signal that this conversation had ended. "Come on. The car is waiting, and Lenora is already downstairs. You know how Lenora is."

I gave up fighting and followed his lead. He was a man focused on one singular thing that night: making an impression. Anniversaries like this didn't come around often, and he'd wanted to make a statement about Rothschild International Acquisitions. A big statement.

We could have celebrated in the ballroom at Rothschild Plaza, but he'd nixed the idea in favor of the best ballroom at New York Athletic, a private club full of old-money, New York somebodies. He wanted to remind everyone in subtle and not-so-subtle ways that we, the Rothschilds, had access and power that most people in New York could only dream about. To help in this mission, he'd hired the best caterer in town, given Lenora a $45,000 budget for flowers, and contracted Jean Guillermo, an event designer, whose credentials included New York Fashion Week, to design tablescapes and room décor destined for their own *Town and Country* spreads. The three of us made an entrance just after eight as a band from Los Angeles played 80s favorites, a throwback to the founding year of his company.

"Your father has really done it," Lenora whispered to me as she took a glass of champagne off a tray carried by a passing waiter. "We've done it. Top of *Page Six* tomorrow. Easily."

I raised my glass to hers. "You should be proud. The flowers are exquisite."

Lenora blushed. "You really think so?"

"Yes," I said, knowing a singular truth about my father—he didn't hand out many compliments. Lenora needed to hear that she'd accomplished her main task. She had good taste, and it showed. "Dad should be pleased. Anyone would be."

A long time ago, I'd resigned myself to a few facts about Dad and the women in his life. He loved women, and the younger the better. Somehow, he thought this made him appear more youthful, even though no one would have mistaken him for a young man. The divorce between him and my mother during my sophomore year at Harvard had been hell. A deep freeze set in between us, something that grew worse when Mom died of breast cancer five years later. I'd blamed him for the unhappiness that settled around her once their ugly separation became public. His second wife hadn't been someone I'd bothered getting to know. Veronica stayed away from me, but remained married to him just long enough to bear my half-brother, Marcus. We'd never gotten along.

But Lenora was different. Time had passed—a lot of it. And I didn't have the energy to take my frustrations out on my father's wives any more. Besides, she probably wouldn't be around long enough to make it worth my time.

"Stop it, Luke." Lenora laughed in between champagne sips. "I know you don't know the difference between tulips and peonies."

"You're right, I don't. But it does look wonderful. Everyone in the city will be talking about this tomorrow." I drank some champagne. "You should be happy. More than happy."

"But you aren't, are you?" She glanced at the other partygoers, many of which seemed focused on filling up the large dance floor in the center of the room. "Of course, I don't want to bring up something like this in the middle of party—"

"No one's paying attention."

"Probably not." Leona stepped closer to me. "You know, in the last few weeks, maybe even months now, your father has become transfixed on the succession of the company. It's all he talks about. All he thinks about."

"I'm not surprised." I took a salmon-and-caviar-covered crostino from another passing tray. It tasted like smoked salt and I put it down on the cocktail table beside us after one bite. "When Dad focuses in on something, he doesn't let it go."

"Of course, he's told me about how he wants you to figure into all of this."

I nodded.

"And for the life of me, I just can't figure you out, Luke." Lenora tilted her head. "He's not asking much, just for you to settle down, to find someone."

"The right someone. Just like *he* did three times."

Lenora blanched, and I immediately regretted my words.

"I didn't mean that."

"No, you did." She put her half-empty champagne flute next to my half-eaten appetizer. "You meant every word, and I get it. I know what's said about me behind my back. I'm your father's third wife. Respect from you isn't something that I expect." She crossed her arms, and it made her cleavage line deepen against the clingy fabric of her lace-covered evening gown. "You can take my advice or leave it. But that's a lot of money on the table, and he's been waiting for years to give it to you. He just wants one thing."

"Assurance that he'll see the Rothschild family live on, so that he can step down from it with confidence."

"That takes a family." Lenora put her hand on my arm. "And you're almost forty."

"I'm not yet thirty-five."

She shrugged. "You know how your father is."

I laughed. I did know how he was. He had never hidden that.

"It's a little ironic to be lectured on this by someone who's three years younger than me."

"Hey, I'm just sick of hearing about it." Lenora raised both hands. "I'd do anything for a little piece and quiet."

Natalie

"Natalie, are you still in the practice room?" Helen called from the studio lobby. "Can I come in?"

"Yes," I said as I rolled up my yoga mat. The last student in my Saturday flow class had just left, and soon, we'd close the studio for the evening. "What's up?"

"Oh, nothing." Helen had a large grin on her face when she walked through the doorway. "Just wondering what you're doing tonight."

I shrugged. "Not a lot."

Truth told, I hadn't been doing much of anything for the last few days besides going to work, running a few miles every night in the neighborhood that surrounded the apartment complex, and binge-watching trash TV.

And thinking about Luke.

"I don't have a lot of plans."

"Which means you're going to spend the whole night on the couch watching on-demand movies and eating popcorn."

"Sounds like a good idea to me, and one that doesn't cost very much." I tucked my mat underneath my arm and breezed past Helen, headed to the large closet where we stored instruction equipment, yoga blocks, straps, and extra merchandise. My mat went on the second shelf. "What do you have in mind?"

I probably could have answered that question myself.

"Well…it's two-for-one margaritas tonight at Sturkey's, and Josh said Keith is coming." She adjusted her ponytail of thinning brown hair. "It's the perfect night to meet him. He's a great guy."

"I don't know—"

"It's not like you're dating anyone else."

True.

"I just don't think—"

"Come on, Natalie." She put a hand on her hip. "What's it going to hurt? It's better than scouring Snap-Date looking for someone."

I winced. SnapDate. The app's IPO had been a huge success, and I'd seen all kinds of articles about the millions the company made when it launched on Wall Street. It was also the night after the anniversary party. Luke would be in New York, finishing his visit. For the hundredth time that day, I wondered if he was enjoying himself.

Probably.

"One night of your life," Helen pointed out. "What's holding you back?"

"Nothing. Absolutely nothing."

Helen let out a tiny squeal. "Great. I'm so excited— this is so perfect. You're finally going to meet Keith! And just think, if you two hit it off—"

"Don't get ahead of yourself." I held up a hand. "It's drinks. That's all."

"It's going to be more than that. You'll see." Helen winked at me, took her phone from the pocket of her zip-up sweatshirt, and sent Josh a text. "All set up," she said after her phone pinged a reply. "Eight thirty. Sturkey's Bar. Be there, and look hot."

Natalie

K eith had frosted tips in his hair and a tattoo that wrapped around his forearm. He sauntered into Sturkey's a few moments after Josh finished his shift, and they clasped hands in a way that told me they'd practiced this special handshake at least a dozen times.

I knew about ninety seconds after meeting him that I wouldn't like him—at least, I wouldn't like him like *that*. No way. No how. Nope. We wouldn't be anything more than friends, and that was a stretch, too. As the four of us sat at a wooden table in the corner of the bar, a sinking feeling filled the pit of my stomach. Look up the word "meathead" in the dictionary, and the definition would have a photo of Keith.

"So, you're the one I've been hearing so much about," Keith said as we looked over the cocktail menu. "The flexible one."

"Keith—come on. Way to make an impression." Helen gave him a chiding half-smile. "She's a yoga queen, though. Better than me."

"That so?" Keith grunted. "I've never tried it. I prefer lifting."

"Damn right." Josh signaled the waiter and ordered us a round of craft beers. I hated beer, but I didn't argue with him. Josh wouldn't have listened, anyway. Since he worked at Sturkey's, he considered himself a connoisseur of liquor, and he always insisted his bar had the best brews on tap in the city. When the drinks arrived, he raised his mug. "To new beginnings."

"New beginnings," echoed the three of us, and we all raised our beers to toast with him.

"I want to dance," Helen said after she downed a large gulp. I put my own drink on the table without taking a sip. "Come on, honey." She stood, and Josh followed her; he let her lead him to the small dance floor at the other end of the room. Seconds later, he wrapped his arms around her, and they swayed to the country song played by The Broken Misfits, a cover band from Delray Beach.

"He'd do anything for her," Keith said.

"She feels the same way about him."

"Strange to see that—he's whupped." Keith over enunciated the word "whupped," dragging it out syllable by syllable.

"How long have you known Josh?"

"Couple years." He ticked off the time on his thick fingers. "Almost four, actually. Long time."

Then he burped. A loud, wet, guttural sound that made one of the women seated at the table behind us turn her head.

Yikes.

"Excuse me." Keith beat his chest a few times with his fist. "Carbonation. Always messes with my acid reflux."

And then he burped again. Louder this time.

"Are you okay?"

I asked this to be polite, and not because I cared. I was already working out a thousand excuses in my head for never seeing this guy again. Helen would be disappointed that her matchmaking efforts had failed, but she'd get over it. Once this night ended, it would be better for everyone.

"I'm fine." Keith grunted for the second time that night. "Fine. No big deal."

"Good," I lied. This night had just begun, and it was already going south.

"Let's order something, sweet cheeks."

I bristled, but he didn't seem to notice.

Instead, Keith slid a menu from between the napkin stand and the ketchup bottle. "What do you like?"

Healthy food. Smoothies. Fruit. Anything that isn't processed. And anything that doesn't involve sitting here with you.

"What would you like to order?"

Keith scanned the menu. "How about buffalo wings?"

"Wings?"

"They have great ones here." Keith closed the menu and replaced it between the ketchup and the napkin holder. "Their sauces are fantastic."

"As fantastic as their beer?"

"Of course. Speaking of which"—he gestured at my glass— "you haven't had any of your beer."

"No, I haven't. I didn't really care for it."

He frowned. "What are you? An alien? Everyone likes it. Beer and wings—that's America."

"Not me. I guess that makes me un-American." I glanced at the dance floor. Helen and Josh had disappeared further into the crowd, and seemed oblivious to anything happening in the bar. I stood from the table. "Excuse me, Keith. I've got to take care of something. I'll be back in a minute."

He protested, but I ignored him, pivoted on my heel, and pushed my way through the growing crowd of twentysomethings and college students. It wasn't lost on me that it was the second time in a week that I'd abruptly left a restaurant. I wouldn't have called that normal, but I didn't care. I just had to get out of there, had to escape the mediocrity that my life had become. I was twenty-five. In debt. Running a yoga studio in a town full of them. And all the men my age seemed like clueless Neanderthals.

Once outside on the sidewalk, I found my phone in the bottom of my purse. I tapped out an "I'm sorry, I just wasn't feeling good" text message to Helen and dropped it back in the bottom of the bag.

Air. I needed air. And a reset on my life.

I walked down the sidewalk, headed in the general direction of the Intercostal Waterway. Sturkey's sat on a side street just off Clematis, one of the main entertainment districts of West Palm Beach. I stumbled through the crowds spilling out of local bars and milling around the sidewalks outside the open-air patios of the restaurants. All around me, the city bustled and burst with the excitement of another balmy Saturday night in the middle of winter.

I barely saw any of it.

When I got to Flagler Park, I finally exhaled, and my shoulders relaxed as I drew closer to the waterfront walkway that lined downtown West Palm Beach. I slowed my pace and took in the peaceful view of the yachts and private boats moored along the waterfront for the winter. Surprisingly, the area closest to the water was almost deserted, and I welcomed that as I sat down on a vacant bench. I just needed to think. I needed space. And most of all, I needed to stop going on horrible dates with men who gave halfhearted apologies for burping in my face.

My phone buzzed a few times, and I felt it vibrate against my stomach, through the cloth of my purse. I didn't have to see it to know who wanted to reach me.

"No," I said to my purse. "I'm not answering you, Helen."

The phone buzzed again.

"I'm not answering you!"

I shifted on the bench and made eye contact with a scruffy man a few benches away. He must have taken this as an invitation, because he got up and made his way over to me.

"Miss, I hate to trouble you, but I'm wondering if you had a little bit extra to spare."

"I…I don't have any money."

"I just need a dollar or some change to help me get a bus fare to Miami." He stopped a few feet in front of me. His eyes sagged, streaks of dirt covered his face, and he smelled like rancid sweat. "It's only a few bucks." The man's voice broke. "I really don't want to trouble you but…"

"It's okay. You're not bothering me." I took another long look at him, wondering when this person had last eaten a decent meal. It had probably been a while. "I don't have much." I opened my purse and fished out my wallet. When I opened it, my heart sank at the sight of five ones and a ten, fifteen bucks that would more than pay for a car ride home. Without them, I'd have to put yet another charge on my credit card.

Still, he needs the money more than me…

"Here, I've got fifteen dollars." I produced the cash and handed it over to him. "That should help."

His jaw went slack, and I knew that he hadn't expected me to give him anything at all. "Oh, wow, miss, that is so kind of you."

"Don't worry about it." I shook my head. "Just have a good night, okay? Take care of yourself."

"I will." He put the money in the front pocket of his pants. "Thank you."

We said goodnight, and he shuffled away, moving along the waterfront. I watched him shuffle away feeling some more of the tension release from my shoulders. It had been a weird night—the weirdest one in a while.

I wanted to go home. I wanted a hot bath. And I wanted a glass of cheap wine.

I was thinking about all of that when the man I'd just given the money to cried out near the edge of the water. His knee gave way and he landed on the concrete, inches away from falling into the Intracoastal Waterway.

"Are you okay?" I yelled as I jumped from the park bench and rushed toward him. "Sir? Are you okay? What happened? Sir—"

When I reached his side, I pulled him away from the concrete lip and onto the pavestones that made up part of the long pathway in the park. He made a few grunting noises and shook a few times as his eyes rolled back into his head.

"Can you hear me? Sir, are you okay? If you can hear me, try to reply…"

He answered me with a few more meaningless, inaudible grunts; nothing he did satisfied me in any way. Whatever had happened to him, I knew it was bad.

Very bad.

I glanced up, my heart racing, and scanned the park. *Shit.* We might as well have been all alone on a deserted island. The closest people were hundreds of feet away and seemed engrossed in their own evening by the water. I looked down at the stranger again, and what I saw put the fear of hell in me. His chest rose and fell in ragged, irregular breaths. At times, he would go long stretches without pulling any air in, and then he would struggle through a staccato of agonizing respirations.

Crap! Is the guy dying?

I fished my phone out of my purse once again. "Hold on," I told him, unsure if he could hear or understand me. "I'm going to call 911."

Still keeping my eyes on him, my hand trembled as I punched a few buttons on my phone and dialed the dispatcher. She asked about our emergency and our location, then told me that an ambulance would be on the way. As instructed, I set my phone on speaker and placed the device on the ground beside me. In between questions from the dispatcher about the man's irregular breathing patterns and her coaching me on performing chest compressions, I kept coaxing him to wake up and talk to me.

"C'mon, c'mon…" I pumped and pumped and pumped on his surprisingly hard chest. My arm muscles ached, and after I don't know how many rounds, sweat beaded on the back of my neck and my lungs burned for air of my own.

Yet I kept enough oxygen aside to beg him to do *some*thing to show me that he'd be all right.

Damn it, *anything*!

But my pleas didn't do much good.

In fact, his breathing slowed to shorter, less frequent gasps, his skin grew sallow under the dim waterfront lamplights, and I didn't feel any sense of relief at all.

Not until I heard the loud sirens of the ambulance, saw the red-and-blue swirls of its lights, and caught a glimpse of the wagon pulling up along the park pathway.

"Miss, can you tell us what's going on?" asked one of the male paramedics as he sprinted over to us. He'd just hopped out of the passenger side of the ambulance.

"I-I don't know." I snatched up my phone, stood, and took a step away from the homeless man so that the EMT could start helping him. I noticed just then how people had been gathering, gawking. But no one had bothered to help me. Not one. "He asked me for money, and then when he walked away, he collapsed. I can't wake him up." My stomach lurched, and a hot flash coursed through me. "Do you think he'll be okay?"

"It's a good thing you called, miss," he said, and turned back to the homeless man.

The other paramedic soon arrived, and he carried a long, red stretcher. I backed away to give them further room to work. I didn't leave completely though, I just kept watching them try to get him help that he clearly needed.

And that's when my phone buzzed for the third time that night. I hadn't even realized that I still clutched it in my left hand.

"Helen, I'm not going to an—" I looked at the screen and stopped short, then punched answer on the screen. "Luke?"

"Hey, Natalie." His voice sounded off kilter and a little less steady than usual. "What's going on?"

"Why did you call me?" I took a seat once again on the bench.

"I just got home from New York," he said. "And I just felt like I needed to call you. I can't stop thinking about the other night and I just…I didn't mean for it to come across that way."

I sighed. "It's fine. It's not a big deal."

"No, I think it is." He paused. "Listen, is everything okay?"

"Yeah, I think so." My answer couldn't have convinced anyone, and I knew it as soon as I said it.

"Did I call at a bad time?"

"Well, I…" My attention focused again on the man, who still had the emergency responders kneeling over him "Actually, I'm at Flagler Park. This homeless guy passed out in front of me and…well, I don't know if he's going to be okay."

"What?" Luke's voice sounded a little sharper.

"They're working on him right now. He's…god, I don't know."

"Did you say you're at Flagler?"

"Yeah." I blew out a large breath. "Right by the waterfront."

"I just left the airport. I'll be right there."

"What? You're coming here?"

Luke didn't answer. He'd hung up.

"We're going to have to put him on the backboard," I heard one of the paramedics say. The comment shook away my thoughts of Luke and brought me back to my immediate concerns about the person who had passed out in front of me.

I got up from my seat and moved back toward the EMTs. "What else can I do to help?"

The growing darkness made it hard for me to see them do their work, but I could still make out the general idea. The first paramedic turned toward me. "Did he say anything strange before he passed out?"

"I don't know." I shook my head. "Nothing out of the ordinary, I guess. He wanted money."

The paramedic and his coworker began to move their patient onto the backboard. "Didn't complain of any chest or stomach pains?"

"No." I shook my head as I played our interaction over again in my mind. "I don't think he's had a shower in a while, and he seemed pretty desperate, but other than that… I can't think of anything."

The two emergency responders stabilized the man's neck with a brace, rolled him onto a backboard then they heaved him onto the stretcher. The second EMT, the larger one, fastened a few of the buckles. "It looks like a heart attack to me," he said to his colleague.

The first EMT grunted in agreement. "He may have hit his head when he fell, too. Likely, at least has a concussion."

"Where are you taking him?" I asked.

"Good Samaritan is the closest," he said.

My thoughts switched to the myriad of hospital bills this man would run up if he had indeed suffered a heart attack and survived. Thousands of dollars. He wouldn't be able to pay them, so someone else would end up with the bills.

The two men finished strapping him to the gurney. They disengaged some latches, raised the gurney into the up position, and rolled him to the ambulance, which already had the backdoors open. Finally, they placed him on the mobile bed in the center of the transport and said a few other things to each other that I couldn't quite catch.

"I'm just—" I murmured, and then felt a hand on my shoulder. I turned around and found Luke standing there. "Oh, my god."

"When I called you, I was just around the corner. A few blocks up the street. It only took a minute to find a parking spot," he said, a smirk pulling at his mouth. "So here I am." He raised his hand as if he wanted to touch my face, but then his hand fell back to his side. "Looks like you've had quite an interesting evening.

"Yes, I have." My attention shifted to the ambulance, which the EMTs were finishing loading up before they left for the hospital. "I think he's going to be okay. I hope so…"

Luke pointed in the direction of the ambulance. "Was it pretty bad? What exactly happened?"

"He asked me for money, I gave it to him." I shrugged, still incredulous about everything that had happened tonight. First the date, then the emergency, and now Luke…

"How much money did you give him?"

"My last fifteen dollars." One technician got in the driver seat of the ambulance, cranked the engine, and flipped on the sirens. "He said he needed money for a bus ticket to Miami." I glanced over at Luke, who wasn't paying attention to the flashing lights or the commotion of the ambulance. Instead, he was engrossed in what I had to say. His eyes were wide, and his lips parted. "Something about the way he spoke to me made me feel bad for him. I believed him. And then when he walked away, he collapsed."

Luke put his hand on my shoulder and stepped closer to me. "You saved that man's life, Natalie."

I waved a hand and looked away. "Anyone else would have done the same thing."

"No, they wouldn't have." His voice softened as he pulled nearer to me. Our gazes connected again, and a spark ignited in my stomach once more, creating a fire that

112

threatened to consume me. "You're amazing, Natalie. Do you know that?"

"Thank you," I said.

"I'm sorry about the other day." Luke lifted his hand again and brushed a few strands of hair out of my face. The softness of his touch only heated the growing warmth in my stomach. "I kept thinking about it in New York. I'm sorry. Let's start over, okay?" He gave me a short bow. "Pretend you just met me."

I cocked my head. "I don't think it works that way, but I forgive you. I'm not mad. In fact, I don't think I ever really was."

His fingers found mine. "You've had quite a night. Do you mind if I take you home?"

"I'd like that a lot."

"Good." He squeezed my hand. "Let's go."

ELEVEN

Natalie

"So…this isn't the way back to my apartment," I said from the passenger seat of the BMW about five minutes later as Luke drove the car across the Royal Park Bridge from West Palm Beach into Palm Beach.

"Oh, it's not?" Luke gave me a sideways glance as he brought the car to a stop at the first light on the island. "My bad. You said go home, so I just thought—"

"Don't act so innocent."

"What? I'm trying to be a nice guy here. I just saved your life."

I laughed. "I wouldn't go that far. But thanks."

"Besides, my place is closer." Luke took his hand off the steering wheel and wrapped it around mine again. "I figured…"

I laughed. "Figured what?"

He shrugged. "I'm trying to be a gentleman here, I promise. So, why don't we just stop there first, and then see what we think?"

I knew better than to argue. In fact, I didn't want to. In comparison to what I'd just had to deal with, Luke and his constricted, strange, gilded life seemed like a dream. And I wanted more of him. Being around him felt like being on a drug. My eyelids seemed heavier, and my muscles relaxed in his presence.

If I wasn't careful, I'd become addicted to Luke Rothschild very fast.

I was still thinking this fifteen minutes later as I sat at his kitchen table with a fresh glass of wine. "You live a beautiful life. That's undeniable."

Luke sat across the table from me. He, too, held a glass of wine. "It's beautiful on the outside, I'll admit that. But I told you, it comes with its own challenges."

"Faye, and what happened to her," I said softly.

He nodded and set his jaw a little tighter.

"I'm sorry, I shouldn't have brought her up again." I glanced away and focused on the tilework of the backsplash for a second. "I know you don't like to talk about her."

"It's okay," Luke said, and the warmth in his voice made me turn my eyes back to him. "I like the fact that you do. Most people, outside my family don't like to bring her up. It's like they're scared to upset me. But you're not, are you?"

"No, but that's because I can be a blunt person. It's just easier in life to call things like they are, sometimes." I studied him. "And your father is another huge challenge, isn't he?"

Luke's handsome mouth moved into a wry smile. "He's certainly one of them, yes."

"Speaking of him, how did the trip to New York go? I thought you'd be staying the whole weekend."

"No, I decided not to. It wasn't simple. It's *never* simple." Luke sipped his wine. "I don't like what New York does to me, I came back earlier than I first expected. It seemed easier to be in Palm Beach than to be stuck dealing with family expectations in a city I hate."

"Hate is a pretty strong word."

He drank some more wine. "Only word that fits."

Something about the wistful expression on Luke's face made me think he wasn't telling me all that he could about whatever had gone on in New York.

"You don't want to talk about it, do you?"

"No," he said evenly.

I looked away again and focused for a moment on a large, abstract, watercolor painting that hung on the kitchen wall above a low set of cabinets. When I glanced back at Luke once more, I swallowed. "Well, I'm sure it can be complicated."

Of course, I didn't understand. How could I?

Luke cleared his throat. "Here's the important thing to remember—it doesn't matter how much money is at stake or what people 'think' about my family's legacy. In the end, it's all about the basics. My father likes control. In fact, he worships it. He thinks if he controls me, he controls his legacy." He eyed me. "You know what? You're really gorgeous, Natalie."

"Don't change the subject." A flush of warmth spread up my neck and face. "But, thank you."

"I bet people tell you that all the time."

"They don't."

"A shame."

My gaze met his. "You should see the kinds of guys that I usually meet. Like the one earlier tonight? Before you found me at the waterfront?" I shook my head as if that would shake the unpleasant memory out of my head. "He was a real winner."

"How?"

"Pretty on the outside, but that's about it." I closed my eyes at the memory. "Nothing underneath the surface. Someone who idolizes himself as much as his daily trips to the gym."

"You don't need guys like that." He got up from the table and moved to the refrigerator, where he offered me another round. When I declined, he refilled his wine and took a drink from his refreshed glass. "You need a real man."

"And that's you?"

"Yes," he said as he sauntered toward me, glass in hand. "Haven't you guessed? That's me."

Luke stopped only when he reached my side, and when he did, he placed his wine on the table, then stroked the edge of my jawline with his index finger. "You're nothing like the other women I've been with in a long time. And I like that."

"I like it, too," I whispered, suppressing a shudder of excitement from his hot touch.

The words had barely escaped my lips before Luke leaned down and kissed me. He crushed his mouth to mine, and it sent a chill through my body. I couldn't stop myself from kissing him back, and I realized in that moment just how much I wanted that from him.

We stayed locked together. The moment was too perfect, too much of a relief. Soon, I stood from the chair so that I'd be able to meet his endless kisses full on, without any distractions. He groaned as I did this, and pulled me into his arms. We embraced like we'd both been waiting to do so for weeks, as if the moment had been building and demanded a release.

"Jesus, Natalie," he breathed against my mouth after a few moments. "I want you. Do you realize that?"

"Good," I replied. "Because I want you, too."

He pulled away a little farther. "I knew I had to have you when I first saw you that afternoon, when I almost hit you with my car."

"I'm glad you didn't hit me. That would have sucked."

He chuckled and ran his hands up and down my exposed arms before stopping at my neck just underneath my hair. "Will you stay the night?"

We both knew what would happen if I did, and he probably could guess that I would. Spending the night with him was a foregone conclusion. Still, I decided to tease him for a moment.

"How badly would you like me to stay?"

Luke pressed his forehead against mine. "Do you really have to ask a question like that? I think you can figure out the answer."

His mouth found mine again, and neither of us held anything back. We melted into each other, and before I knew it, he was leading me through the house, and up the wide staircase. "My room is on the left," he said when I reached the catwalk landing that crossed over the expansive living room and united the two major wings of the house.

As soon as we arrived at the doorway, he lifted me up, then carried me to the bed and laid me down on the silky duvet. Luke's master bedroom featured a California king bed, a few lounge chairs, and an open area that I assumed ended at the master bathroom. Two large pieces of modern art complemented the minimalist décor.

"I'm going to make you scream," he murmured. "Like no one else has before."

"Good," I said, already losing myself against his touch. "Because I need you to fuck me. Now."

He lowered his head and growled in my ear. "Do you know what you just said?"

"Yes. And I meant it."

Luke must have taken me at my word, because his lips covered mine again, and the kisses intensified as a fever built between us. His hands seemed like they were everywhere, and nowhere all at once. When I couldn't take it any longer, I untied the straps of my dress and pushed it down, leaving my collarbone and the top of my chest exposed. Luke followed my lead and traced a pathway down my body with his lips. When he arrived at my breasts, he massaged one with his hand and drew the other into his mouth.

I drew in a sharp breath. "Oh, god."

Luke played with my breasts for a while, then turned his attention further south. He pulled the dress down my hips and off my legs, taking my underwear with the garment. He explored my ribs and the soft swell of my stomach before stopping just underneath my belly button. As I lay naked before him, he spread my legs and slipped his index finger inside of me. I rose up to meet him, and the warmth inside me built as he stroked in and out of my core. He kissed me a few times as he pleased my body, and then his mouth traveled to the apex of my thighs.

I groaned again.

"You are so beautiful."

His tongue teased me where, moments before, his fingers had been. I relaxed against the bed and took in the ecstasy of it all, letting the moment wash over me like a smooth ocean wave. He tasted every part of me, and when I couldn't take it any longer, I let go, giving in to my feelings and the utter rawness of how he seemed to know where I yearned to be touched. Before I knew it, he was naked, too.

"Are you ready for more?" Luke whispered in my ear. "Because I'm not finished."

He found a condom in the nightstand and put it on, then moved us underneath the duvet. The cold sheets made me shiver, and the heat of his body seemed hotter. I craved every part of him, and I begged him to take me.

He responded by starting a long trail of kisses from my ear to my stomach before he entered me with a decisive thrust.

We moved together in the bed, becoming as one. The energy between us continued to build, and he said my name over and over as we elongated the chemistry. I needed it to never end; our connection seemed to strengthen with every second and every touch. Finally, I reached the edge just before he did, and we sank together into the bed, a tangle of arms and legs.

"That was amazing," I managed in between deep breaths while I tried to still the pounding in my heart and lungs.

"You have no idea how sexy you really are." He kissed me. "And yes, that was unforgettable."

Luke smoothed the sheets and arranged the duvet around us, then he lay on his side and wrapped one arm around me. His hand settled in between my breasts. We fell asleep in the stillness, the faint sound of the evening tide in the distance.

TWELVE

Luke

For the first time in months, maybe years, I woke up knowing the name of the woman in the bed beside me. What a miracle.

As usual, I opened my eyes first, and I studied Natalie as she got the last few moments of sleep before my alarm sounded. When it went off, she yawned and turned toward me.

"What time is it?"

"Seven forty-five." I switched off the ringing.

"Hmm." She molded herself against me and, for once, I didn't consider asking her to leave as I had other women. Instead, I wanted to slow down the morning as much as I could.

"What time do you have to be at the yoga studio?" I asked into her hair.

"Never. It's always closed on Sundays." She propped herself on her elbow and looked down at me. "I have the whole day to do…nothing."

"No plans?"

She shook her head.

"Good." I reached up and cupped her face, then rose to kiss her cheek. "Do you want to spend the day with me?"

She arched her eyebrow. "And what do you have in mind?"

I kissed her again. "I can think of a few things."

"You can?" Her eyes softened, and she moved, opening herself to me.

Hungrily, I covered my mouth with hers. A small moan escaped her lips, and before I knew it, we were entwined in a mix of desire, emotions, and raw chemistry.

"I've never met anyone like you," I murmured as I shifted over the top of her. I pushed away the bedsheets and took time to savor every part of her curvy body. I kissed her chin, the soft skin of her neck, her elegant collarbone, and the upper swell of her warm breasts. When I reached her hard nipples, I tasted the sweetness of each one before I skimmed my lips down to her creamy core, to the apex of her thighs.

I stopped and connected my gaze with hers. "I thought I was dead before I met you," I said. "But now I realize that I'm just starting to live."

"I feel that way, too." Her breath came out in jagged gasps. "I know it's crazy, but I'm falling for you."

I climbed higher, walking my hands on either side of her hips, waist, and shoulders, and then I lowered my weight on top of her. We connected, and I entered her again, cherishing this moment of raw closeness that felt like nothing I'd encountered in the last few years. I couldn't deny my hunger for her, or the maddening sensation of having her silky body entwined with mine, her long legs wrapped around me, her arms clinging to my neck, the scent of her musky arousal wafting up to stir my needs and make me harder. And the way she rocked with me—the snugness of her slick channel stroking me while her full breasts teased my chest. Hell, she *must* have been made for me—only me. I'd never had sex like this.

Never.

A short time later, we donned bathrobes and padded downstairs to find breakfast. George, my house manager, already sat at the large kitchen table, polishing a few pieces of crystal. When we walked in, his eyes widened, and he stood.

"Mr. Rothschild, I wasn't aware that you had a guest." George took a few steps toward the kitchen counter.

"That's quite all right." I held up a halting hand.

"Perhaps I could start a pot of coffee?"

"Yes, I'd like that. And Natalie will be joining me for breakfast."

If George had an opinion about this, it didn't show on his face. Instead, he located a frying pan in the drawer underneath the stove. "How about two frittatas, Mr. Rothschild?"

"Sounds excellent."

Twenty minutes later, Natalie and I sat at the patio table overlooking County Road and the beach. We both had

124

coffee and half-eaten servings of spinach-and-ham frittatas in front of us, and I admired how the sun captured the natural highlights in her ash-blonde hair.

She grinned at me over the rim of her mug. "You keep staring at me."

"I do."

"Why?"

"Because you have a beautiful face."

She wrinkled her nose.

"Still beautiful."

She squinted her eyes and stuck out her tongue.

"You can't make yourself look ugly. It's impossible."

"Oh, it's possible. You should see me after a long night of drinking and no sleep."

"Maybe some time, I will."

She sipped her coffee, then placed the cup on the table beside her meal. "I just realized—we've slept together, and I know almost nothing about you. Well, nothing besides what Helen found on Google."

"What do you want to know?"

She ticked off a list on her fingers. "Favorite food?

"Guacamole."

"Color?"

"Black."

"Band?"

"Radiohead."

"Vacation spot?"

"Tough one." I thought about it. "The Amalfi Coast."

She cocked her head. "Where's that? I've never heard of it."

"It's a stretch of coast in Western Italy." I drank some coffee. "And it's gorgeous."

"I'll bet." She glanced down at the table.

"Have you ever been abroad, Natalie?"

As soon as I asked the question, I felt stupid. I knew the answer before she spoke it: no. She hadn't.

"Only in my dreams," she said when she lifted her gaze again.

"That's a shame. Maybe we'll change that sometime."

We regarded each other for a moment, and I realized how much I wanted that idea to come true, how much I wanted to make those kinds of memories with Natalie. I could see it in my mind—the look of wonder on her face as we took in the sweeping clifftop views so famous in that region, the way she'd laugh when we dined at my favorite restaurant there.

I could do this. I knew it. I could do it with her.

"Okay," she said, breaking me away from the daydream. "Do you have a habit you wish you could break?"

"Biting my fingernails." I examined my left hand, which had a hangnail that very moment. I picked at it, and made a mental note to cut it later. "I do that when I'm nervous. And you?"

She ticked through the list. "Tacos, blue, The Chainsmokers, I don't know, and biting the inside of my cheek. I do that when I'm stressed out, which is often."

"There you go." I speared another piece of frittata with my fork. "Now we know each other. Which is good, since we're exchanging bodily fluids on a regular basis."

She wrinkled her nose, then laughed. "That's one way to put it."

I ate the bite of egg pastry. "You know, George probably wonders what's going on. I don't let a lot of women eat breakfast with me."

"So, I should consider myself special, huh?"

"Something like that. None of my staff have ever met anyone since Faye. I haven't allowed it."

She knitted her brow. "How many people work for you?"

"Let's see…" I wiped my mouth with my napkin. "Not including George—three. I have two gardeners, a housekeeper, and him."

Her eyes widened.

"What?" I ate another bit of breakfast. "Does that bother you?"

"No…yes. I don't know. It's just strange." She laughed to herself. "Well, it sounds strange to me. But I guess it shouldn't come a shock. I mean, you are—"

"What? Rich?" I put down my fork. "In a way."

She furrowed her brow. "In *every* way."

"Being rich is relative." I wiped my mouth on my napkin. "And all the money in the world doesn't matter if you don't have people in your life that you actually care about." I paused. "So, up until recently, I'd say I was pretty poor."

Her jaw went slack. She didn't have to tell me what she was thinking—I could already guess.

I drank some more of my lukewarm coffee. "Enough about me. Tell me about you—I want to hear it all."

She sipped her own coffee, regarding me over the rim with wide blue eyes. "Trust me, you don't."

"Try me," I whispered.

She nodded a few times, as if mulling it over in her head what she'd say next. "It's hard. It's not…it's not easy managing a small business, and we can't ever get ahead. Aunt Helen and I are at the studio six days a week, and we do what we can, but the competition is fierce Whatever isn't going to our basic expenses goes right back into the studio, and lately business has been bad." She looked away and focused on the beach for a beat. "It's a grind. Plus, I have all these student loans…"

"What would you do if you didn't have them?" I asked. "The student loans, I mean."

She looked away for a moment, then focused back on me. "I'd probably open my own business. Something just for me."

"Like what? A boutique? A yoga studio?"

She laughed without humor. "It isn't worth thinking about. Not with all this debt. I can't…I can't afford to focus on things that will never happen."

"I can help you with the debt."

She shook her head. "You mean with the million dollars? I already told you how I feel about that. No deal."

"Yes, I know that—I know where you stand. I'm talking about just in general. I don't mind helping out, if you need it."

"Thanks, but I can make it on my own." She looked at her watch. "Oh, my god, I didn't realize what time it was." She stood from the table. "You know, my aunt is probably wondering what's going on with me after last night. I should at least call her."

She left the patio for less than ten minutes, and when she came back, everything had changed. She wore her dress from the night before, and a frown darkened her gorgeous features.

"What's wrong?" I stood, more out of instinct than anything else.

"It's… She wants me to meet her at the studio. It's important."

"What's the problem?"

"She won't say. She just wants me to meet her there."

Natalie

Luke drove me back to my apartment, so I could get my car—I didn't want my aunt asking too many questions about why I hadn't driven myself to the studio. When he pulled his BMW into the parking lot in front of my meager building, he skimmed his palm along my knee, sending a pleasant shiver up my thigh.

"Can I see you again tomorrow? Do you have anything planned?"

"Sure, I don't have much on the schedule."

I glanced down at his hand, and the memory of the night before pulsed through me once again. I'd just had the best sex of my life. No doubt. I didn't want to leave this man's presence, but I had to. Helen had sent me six text messages, called twice, and left one voicemail, all of which was very unlike her. I needed to figure out what was going on, and why she sounded so frantic.

"There's a gala happening at the Phillips estate on the south end of the island that night. It's one of those very silly events—a lot of money being raised by some very fussy and self-important people. I care about the charity, though, so I'm going. In fact, that reception we attended at Nicalao's was tied to this ball." Luke grazed his hand from my knee to my brow, and then pushed some hair away from my face. "Will you be my date?"

"I don't have—"

"I know. You don't have a dress." He cocked his head. "And there's probably not enough time for me to take you shopping on Worth Avenue for one."

"No," I said, thinking again about my aunt's messages. I had a feeling that whatever she had to say would take up most of the rest of the day.

"Hmm." Luke snapped his fingers. "Why don't you go online and order something from wherever you'd like? You can overnight it, and I'll pay for it."

"No, I can't—"

"It's a gift, Natalie. Nothing more. Nothing attached to it at all." He placed his hand on my arm as if to drive home that point. "I'll text you my AmEx number when I get back to the house."

I eyed him, still a little skeptical. "The same AmEx card I gave back to you?"

He nodded. "I figure you didn't write down the numbers."

"Nope." I smiled. "Paying for it is awfully generous of you. Very trusting."

"I think you've proven that your trustworthy, Natalie," he whispered.

We kissed, and the fire reignited between the two of us, not that it had ever really died down. This man wasn't like any of the other men I'd ever dated. Not at all.

Oh, god, I really *was* falling for him. Hard.

After Luke and I said goodbye, I got in my own car and drove to the studio. In the lobby, Aunt Helen sat waiting for me on the bench across from the main check-in desk. A white piece of paper and an opened envelope lay on the wood next to her. She had her arms crossed and her lips pulled tight. She didn't get up when I walked in the door.

"What's going on?" I didn't even bother greeting her because I knew from her expression that whatever she had to say wouldn't be pleasant. Easier to just get right to it.

"Sit down," she ordered. "You need to sit down for this one."

I took a seat on the bench opposite hers. "Okay. Tell me."

"I got the mail this morning"—she picked up the paper— "and I found *this* in between the stacks of catalogs and junk ads. I almost missed it." She sniffed. "Thank god I didn't."

"What's the—?"

She handed the paper to me and my breath caught in my throat. No. No way. This couldn't be true; this couldn't be happening. Not now. Not to us.

And yet, it was.

"Eviction? What?" I looked up from the paper and my gaze met Helen's. "But our lease here at the studio isn't up for another six months."

"They're giving us thirty-days' notice." Helen sighed. "And the new owner activated the early termination clause." She slumped against the wall behind the bench. "Of course, when I signed the papers, that's not something that I ever thought about."

"Oh, my god." I gulped. "How is this happening?"

"I've been asking myself the same thing for the last hour." She buried her face in her hands. "And I can't figure out what I'm going to do."

"What are they doing with this place if they don't want a yoga studio here?"

She looked up from her hands. "The new owner— some trust called RCS, LLC—plans on turning this whole development into mixed use. He wants to tear down this strip mall. A multimillion-dollar project."

"I haven't heard about it." I glanced at the paper again. "And he's giving you two grand to go away. How generous." I didn't bother to hide my sarcasm or annoyance. Who did this person think they were? They obviously didn't have any kind of attachment to West Palm Beach, or the small businesses that made up the heart of this community.

"Some people would probably say they are being more than kind. They don't have to give us money to leave." Helen shrugged. "I Googled RCS, LLC, and I didn't find anything except incorporation papers in Delaware. Nothing else. Nada."

"What are you going to do?"

"I don't know." Her emotions caught in her throat. "Just when I was thinking we could turn this place around, and that we might have a chance, this happens."

"We're screwed, aren't we?

"I think so."

As I gripped the bench, I started thinking about all the bills that would mount at the end of the month, all the things we wouldn't be able to pay because of this happening—my rent, Helen's rent, my student loan, my credit cards…to say nothing of the membership refunds we'd have to give…we *were* screwed. Royally screwed. More than that—*we were fucked.*

"Shit." I groaned as the dollar signs crowded in my head. Even if I tried to pay off all my debts, I wouldn't be able to. Not even close.

"Shit is right." My aunt sighed. "We're never going to get out from underneath this. And I still have almost fifteen grand outstanding on the loan that I took out to start this place."

"Plus, all of the other bills."

"I know." Her voice broke. "And I don't know how I'm going to pay for it. I don't know what to do."

My thoughts drifted to Luke, and what he'd said that morning at breakfast. Twice since I'd know him, he'd offered to bail me out. Heck, he'd even gone a step further than that—he'd wanted to pay me a million dollars to pretend to be his fiancée in front of his dad. Maybe he'd still take me up on the offer?

If he did, we'd have more than a fighting chance.

"I just don't know how we're going to figure this out." Helen's heavy voice brought me back to reality.

"You will—*we* will," I said. "I promise."

THIRTEEN

Natalie

"I found a dress," I told Luke when I called him on the phone later that afternoon. I tried to sound upbeat and cheerful, even though I didn't feel that way at all. "It's gorgeous. You're going to love it."

"Can't wait." I could almost hear Luke smiling through the phone. "What does it look like?"

"It's a Le Petite Chambordeaux." I knew I butchered the name as I said it, but I willed myself to get through it. If I'd bought the body con dress retail, it would have cost me more than I made in three weeks. I forced myself not to think about that. "It will be here overnight, and they said delivered by no later than noon."

"Perfect. Do you need someone to do your hair and makeup?"

I laughed into the phone. "Let me guess. You know someone for that, too?"

"You could say that. My friend Aaron uses a woman over at Andres' Salon. He likes it there. Call over there and see if Tonya can work you in." He paused. "And I'll pay for that, too."

"Again, I don't think I deserve this." I stretched out on the futon in my apartment, which doubled as my couch and bed. "You're being too kind."

A moment of silence passed between us again, and my thoughts wandered back to what really bothered me. I had no idea how I would pay for anything if he didn't agree to give me money. My credit would be ruined, and I'd probably never get a credit card, mortgage, or bank loan again. I'd have to go back to Kissimmee, and only god knew what kind of work I'd be able to find there. Maybe I'd be able to drive a car for hire. Maybe I'd be able to work as a barista. Or maybe I could get a job working for Mickey Mouse…

"What's really going on?" Luke's question brought my attention back to the phone call.

I cleared my throat. "What do you mean?"

"You sound distracted."

"I do?"

"Yes. Whatever it is—if there's anything I can do, please tell me."

I started to tell him the truth, then thought better of it. It still wasn't the right time to bring up all the problems facing Aunt Helen and me. "I'll let you know. Let's just concentrate on tomorrow night."

"Consider it done. I'll set up your appointment."

Tonya had a last-minute cancelation at four the following day, so a half hour before the appointment, I drove over to the island, parked my car on a side street, and checked in to the salon, which featured long rows of tan chairs overlooking The Brazilian Court Hotel's interior courtyard full of palm trees and flowers. The receptionist offered me a glass of chardonnay, and Tonya regarded me through the large mirror in front of her styling booth.

"What are we doing today?" She picked up a few strands of my hair and twisted her mouth to one side. "Luke said you need makeup and hair for the Children's Fund Gala?"

"That's right." I exhaled, regretting my decision to show up at the salon in yoga pants and a gray zip pullover. I didn't appear as polished as the rest of the clients in the room. "I need something to complement my dress. It's designer—Le Petite Chambordeaux." I mispronounced the name again, but if Tonya noticed, she didn't flinch. "Black."

"Body con?" She laughed once. "Not that they make much of anything else."

I nodded as if I knew this already, even though I didn't. "It's tight and flairs out below the knee. The top has cap sleeves and is sheer across the neckline."

"Sounds beautiful." She continued examining my hair. "Any jewelry?"

"No. I was thinking of keeping it simple to show off the dress."

Plus, I don't own any expensive jewelry…

"Simple is always better." Tonya took a hairbrush from the middle of the beautician tool belt around her waist. "Earlier today, I heard a few people talking about the gala. Sounds like it's going to be almost as big as the

137

International Red Cross Ball. Twelve hundred people? Something like that."

"Wow." I hadn't thought about the size of the event; I'd been so focused on trying to keep my emotions in check after the bad news about Yoga Ohm. Twelve hundred was a lot of people.

"And Luke Rothschild is a big part of tonight. You know that, right? They owe him a lot."

"They do?"

"Yes, he's…" Tonya grinned, showing off perfectly straight teeth. "Anyway, most women around here would kill to go with him to this."

"He's a great guy."

"Can't disagree there." She began brushing my hair, working through a few of the tangles in the back. "You have beautiful hair. Is the color natural?"

"Yes, I don't really do much to it." I couldn't think of the last time I'd had it cut—couldn't really afford that, either.

She stopped brushing my hair and grinned at me again, meeting my gaze once more in the mirror. "I think with a little bit of work, we'll have you looking perfect for tonight. This gala won't know what hit it."

Luke

W hat I saw when Natalie answered the door took my breath away—and for a moment, I considered skipping the gala altogether in favor of throwing her on the futon and having my way with her for the rest of the night.

She looked *that* gorgeous.

My eyes roamed over her body, the dress, the way the light caught the tendrils of her hair...

"What are you looking at?" she asked when it became obvious I was at a loss for words.

"You," I said. "I'm looking at you."

"Good." Natalie stepped through her doorway and shut it behind her, then locked. It. "Tonya does fantastic work."

"It's not her. It's all you."

"Do you really like it?" She stepped away from me and looked down the length of her body. "The dress works?" The long, black gown accentuated her small hips and the swell of her bust. Natalie paired it with nude heels, long diamond earrings, and a small red clutch that matched her lipstick. Her hair tumbled down one shoulder, swept to the side in a long cascade of curls.

She could have walked any red carpet and dominated.

"That dress does more than just work. It defines every curve of your body." I pulled in my lower lip. "God, I want to be inside you right now."

She shook her head. "Nope. Not yet. We've got a gala to go to."

"Too bad." I closed the space between us and put my mouth to her ear. She smelled like roses and jasmine. "I could make you come five ways from Sunday."

I imagined that Natalie's delicate flesh at the apex of her thighs swelled at my touch, and I knew my words were turning her on.

"Who needs a gala when I've got you?"

"Later, Luke." Natalie gave me a quick kiss. "Some things are worth waiting for, right?"

We had about a twenty-minute drive from her apart-ment to the Phillips estate, and I could hardly stand it as I drove. She was too gorgeous, too sensual, and too right-in-front-of-me. I wanted her, and when the drawbridge raised on the Southern Bridge, trapping us on it so a few yachts and a fishing boat could pass on the Intercostal Waterway underneath, I got my chance.

My hand found her knee, right where it met the slit on her dress. Her bare legs felt smooth and moisturized.

"Hey there, killer," she whispered. "What do you think you're doing?"

"We're not going anywhere for a little while." I threw the car into park. "What do you *think* I'm doing?"

"Whatever it is, I like it."

"Good." I jerked my chin toward the side of her seat, closest to the passenger door. "Lean your seat back." My gaze met hers. "Now."

She complied and elongated her body on the seat.

"Spread your legs."

Natalie hesitated.

"You heard me," I ordered. "Do it."

"You're in control, huh?"

"While we're on this bridge, I am. And I get what I want in life."

She nodded, then adjusted her feet on the floorboard of the car and relaxed a little further. "Go for it, then."

I pushed the heavy fabric of her dress to one side and walked my fingers up her knee, then her thigh. When I reached the seam of her panties, she groaned and opened herself up to my touch. I hooked my index and middle finger around the edge, then slipped them underneath. Gently, as we waited for the boats to pass and the bridge to reopen to traffic, I massaged her clit.

"You like that?" I asked as I increased the speed of my fingers, knowing that I only had a limited time to work her over. The bridge usually stayed drawn for less than ten minutes, and I wanted to make her come before we drove the final way into Palm Beach. "That what you want?"

"Yes," she murmured. "Please...don't stop."

I moved one finger from her clit to deep inside her as I heightened the sensation. Now I had control of her, inside and out, and damn, what a charge it gave me. I wanted to give this woman maximum pleasure, and she wanted it, too, moving her hips with me as we drew closer and closer to the apex

"Come on." I leaned over and brushed my lips against her ear. "You know you need this. Give yourself over to it..."

"Yes." Natalie gripped the sides of the seat. "I do..."

I nibbled on her earlobe as I massaged her deepest place, taking in the floral scent of her perfume and the elegant way the curls of her hair framed her sharp chin. Natalie Johnson had a way about her; I didn't think she even really knew it.

"You're almost there," I said against her ear. "Come on, baby. Come for me…"

And then she did.

She bucked against my forearm, then let out a moan and shuddered against me, coming in ecstasy just as the drawn part of the bridge began to lower in front of us. While she gave herself over to the orgasm, I slipped my fingers out of her and put the car into drive. The vertical section of the bridge settled into place and the cars in front of us moved forward.

"You okay?"

She gave me an inaudible answer.

"Perfect," I said, satisfied not only by my handiwork, but by her willingness to let me please her in a way that seemed both public and private. "That's one way to start an evening."

"It is." She straightened her dress but didn't raise her seat.

"We could skip the party."

"And do what?"

"I can think of a few things."

She grinned. "Nope. I'm all ready to go. This is a big night, right?"

"Okay, you win," I said as I tapped the accelerator and gave the car some gas. "We've got an entrance to make."

FOURTEEN

Natalie

You couldn't live in Palm Beach County and not hear about the Highball, the Phillips family estate. People alternated between loving it and hating it, mostly because they had strong opinions about its owner, Roman Phillips, some minor Europe aristocrat who'd made most of his money in semi-shady real estate dealings. To me, though, it was always one of those fabulous places that I thought I'd never get a chance to see on the inside. A place I'd driven by more than once, but not a place for me.

And yet, that night, I walked in to the party on Luke Rothschild's arm.

He pulled the car up to the valet stand just beyond the wrought-iron gate of the estate and hopped out as fast as he could, greeting me with an extended hand a half second after the attendant helped me out of the car. I smoothed my dress and hooked my arm around Luke's.

"Do I look flushed?"

"You look great." He kissed me on the cheek. "A little...glowing...maybe."

Our gazes met, and we exchanged a conspiratorial look. Getting pleasured in the car on the Southern Bridge was a new one, I had to admit that. A very new one. Not that I'd refuse the chance to do it again if Luke offered.

"Right this way," said a man in a tuxedo. He led us up a few stairs and into a two-story living room that could have been straight out of the Palace at Versailles. I'd never seen so much gold leaf or marble in my life.

"It's overwhelming, isn't it?" Luke guided me across the room.

"It's..."

"Gaudy." Luke leaned into me. "Roman Phillips is gaudy. Always has been. Always will be."

"It's still gorgeous, though."

Luke laughed. "In a certain kind of way."

As more people filed into the living room, he stopped to shake hands with a few of them, and introduced me. In fact, most of the people arriving seemed to want to make sure he noticed them.

"You're very popular," I murmured to him when we had another alone moment.

He waved a hand, and the corners of his mouth turned down. "I wouldn't call it that at all."

I stifled a laugh, surprised at how unfazed all of this made him. This whole place was bizarre—to say the least. "You act like you've seen this before."

"Well, I have, in a way. It's not... You know what? You're right. I shouldn't take this for granted. We're lucky to be at a party like this, on a night like this." He plucked up a glass of champagne from a passing waiter, handed it to me, and snatched another for himself. "Cheers."

"Cheers."

We raised our glasses.

"To...building bridges." The corners of Luke's eyes crinkled, and I knew he was thinking about what we'd just shared on the bridge. I kept thinking about it, too. "How does that sound? Bridges."

"To building bridges."

We clinked glasses and drank a sip before Luke led me past a bar stocked full of premium liquor shots, and into an ornate ballroom that doubled as the silent auction area for the event. Across a handful of tables, I saw auction items going for thousands of dollars—two vacation villas in the South of France, a diamond bracelet from Van Cleef and Arpels, a professional shopping getaway in New York City, a set of four box seats at the Super Bowl, a signed Andy Warhol print, and more. I shuddered when I added up the projected values of just a few of the items. I could have paid off my student loans, cut down my credit cards, and saved the business with the cost of just three of them.

Speaking of which...

"What's wrong?" Luke stood beside me, reading a paragraph on a placard about a wine trip to Sicily. The trip included a private stay at a boutique hotel, dinner with a private chef, and the rental of a small yacht for sailing around the island.

"Nothing."

He slipped his hand into mine and squeezed it. "I don't buy that."

"It's…" I looked over at him. "We got some bad news the other day at the yoga studio." I knew I had Luke's full attention, and I sucked in a deep breath. I hadn't planned on telling him this at the start of the evening, but I couldn't hold it in anymore. After all, like my mother often said, bad news didn't get any better with age. "Someone bought out the strip mall, and all the businesses have to close. We have less than a month to get out. No appeal. No chance to change anyone's mind. Nothing."

"Oh, my god."

"It's terrible." Shaking my head, I looked away from him and focused on the rest of the crowd as people browsed the auction. If I kept my attention on them, and not on Luke, maybe I wouldn't start to cry. "We have no clue what we're going to do. None whatsoever."

"Surely you can contact the new owner. Work something out? Maybe see if there's an appeal process…"

"No. Aunt Helen looked up the new owner. It's some LLC registered in Delaware —a bunch of initials. Probably a shell company or something like that." My shoulders slumped as I again realized the heaviness of the situation once again. "The eviction notice came from a real estate attorney in Miami, and when she called them, they didn't give her much information, except to say that the new owners have plans for the area that don't include a yoga studio like ours."

"Jesus."

"I have no idea how we're going to pay the bills from all of this." A server walked by with a few shots of rum on

146

a silver tray. I grabbed one and downed it in a single gulp. "Between the bank loan and my credit cards…"

Luke released my hand, then gripped my upper arm, stopping me midsentence. "Let me take care of it. Let me help you."

"But—"

"My offer still stands."

I exhaled. "Well, I was thinking about what you said about the contract. If you still want me to—"

"Forget the contract. That was before…when I didn't know you as well as I do now." His gaze locked mine. "Whatever you need, I can help you. I don't care about money—I have enough of it. How much is left on the bank loan for the business?"

"Twenty-seven thousand. Helen secured it from Wells Fargo."

"And your debts?"

"Twenty-one." I shook my head, thinking about how bitter it tasted to admit the full sum. "Just over twenty-one thousand."

"I'll pay if off. No problem. We can do it next week."

"Are you—maybe we shouldn't do this," I said, but in a way, I didn't mean it. Luke was giving me exactly what I needed, but I didn't want to come across like I'd expected it. That didn't feel right. "It's too generous."

"Trust me." He nodded at the table, displaying the Italy trip. "If I can afford to bid on that trip or one of the necklaces in this room, I can afford to pay off your bank loan and your debts owed." He moved his hand up my arm and cupped my chin. "So why don't you let me?"

A moment passed between us. This was too easy, but I already knew my reply.

"Thank you," I said. "You don't know how much this means to me, and I probably can't ever pay you back."

"You don't have to," Luke said. "And I don't even want you to try." He wavered as if he wanted to kiss me, but he didn't.

Instead, a pot-bellied man in an ill-fitting tuxedo tapped Luke on his arm. Luke turned, and his jaw went slack. Only then did I see the resemblance and take in my first sight of the curvy, much younger woman hanging off the other man's arm.

"Dad?" Luke's eyes widened.

"I'd ask you what you're doing here," Luke's father said. "But I already know the answer."

I couldn't remember the last time my father had been in Palm Beach. Years. Certainly, before Faye's death. Growing up, we came to the island many times, but my first stepmother loved it more than him, and my father gave it up once the ink dried on the papers ending their marriage. After she exited his life, he sold the house he owned on Australian Avenue, and the yacht he'd kept tied to a slip on the Intercostal. He never acted like he wanted to return.

So, I didn't bother to hide my shock about seeing him at the gala that night.

"What are *you* doing here?" I blurted.

"What everyone does when they're in Palm Beach?" A half-grin pulled at my father's lips. "Enjoying the good life. Raising money for 'charity.'" I bristled at the way my father said the world "charity", but he didn't seem to notice. Instead, he turned to Natalie, extending his hand. "And you are?"

"Natalie."

They shook.

"So, I take it that you're one of my son's…friends."

"That's one way to put it."

"These days, my son has *a lot* of friends." My father shook his head. "Perhaps you've heard of his illustrious reputation."

"I have."

My father's gaze met mine, then Natalie's. A smirk curled his upper lip. "And you're okay with that?"

I stepped close to Natalie, suddenly feeling more than a little bit protective of her. She didn't know the kind of man my father could be when he wanted to make a point. "She is. And really, do we have to do this here?" I turned to Lenora. "Wonderful to see you again."

"You, too, darling." She moved forward to kiss me on the cheek, and when we finished embracing, she glanced at Natalie. "And so fantastic to meet you, as well. What a big night for Luke."

"Big night?" Natalie cocked her head. "What do you mean, big night?"

Lenora looked at me, then back at Natalie. "The award, of course."

"What award?"

"The one for—"

"It's nothing. *Nothing.*" I gave Lenora a look, and she didn't bother finishing her sentence. I placed my hand on the small of Natalie's back. "I think they're serving appetizers by the pool. May I get you one, Natalie?"

"Certainly," she said.

The two of us said goodbye to my father and Lenora. A few minutes later, Natalie and I had a place at a cocktail table draped with a black linen cloth. About ten feet away from us, the rectangular indoor pool glowed with white lights that set off the tropical landscaping. Lenora and my father stood across on the opposite side, engrossed in conversation with David Clarke, a billionaire investor in Hollywood films, and May Jones, David's new fiancée. Most of the partygoers had moved outside, and a few dancers from Miami performed salsa routines on a small stage at the edge of the pool.

"What award?" Natalie asked after taking a miniature tuna tartare off the tray of a passing server. She popped it in her mouth. "Tell me."

"It's hardly an award." I cleared my throat. "Just something they do for the donors sometimes."

"And you're a big one, right?" She cocked her head. "An important one."

"Everyone in here is." I gestured at the crowd, a blur of evening gowns and perfectly pressed tuxedos. "That's how Palm Beach works."

Natalie took another canape, this time a bite-sized slice of brie cheese wrapped in puff pastry. "I've heard." She bit into the pastry.

"I'm sorry about my father. He can be a little— blunt."

"You can be, too."

I laughed. "Touché."

"Honestly, there is no need to apologize." She finished her appetizer. "You should meet mine. He's worse."

"Tell me about him." The words stunned me—I hadn't made that request to any woman since Faye. But Natalie was different than all the rest of them. I wanted to know everything about her, every small fact about her family, her childhood, and her life.

Natalie meant something to me.

She shrugged. "My dad is hardly in my life. My parents divorced when I was three, and he moved to Jacksonville, where he works as a commercial real estate agent. My mom tries her best to stay away from him. Says he's toxic. I honestly don't know. He never acted too interested in getting to know me beyond just the surface."

"That must have been so hard for you—the divorce." I took her hand in mine, and a smidgen of the pain and rejection she must have felt seemed to permeate into me. "If it was anything like my parents...divorce can be hell."

"It was horrible. Disgusting. They did everything they could to hurt each other, even when there was no money at stake." She raised her eyebrow. "Of course, I've read a little about what happened to your parents."

I nodded. "When it happened, the newspapers in New York wrote about it on and off for year."

The corners of her mouth turned down. "I'm sorry, Luke."

"I came to terms with the fact that my father is colorful. Some men trade in their cars every few years. He does that with women."

"And you? People say that you're the same way... when it comes to women, at least."

"I was." I cleared my throat. I had a past, and I knew it. "But recently, I've started to realize that's no way to live."

She opened her mouth to reply, but then Grace Andrews, the co-chair of the event, called out to the crowd over the PA system and asked everyone to move into the grand ballroom for dinner at the program.

I offered Natalie my elbow. "We'll finish this conversation later."

We followed a long line of partygoers through a series of double doors and into a room that easily fit hundreds of people. Circular tables filled the space, and each one featured a large centerpiece of blue flowers that offset gold-rimmed china and the first course of our meal. I placed an arm around Natalie's waist and led her to Table 5, located in the center section of the room. We found two open seats and took our places.

"Wow," she whispered. "This is beautiful."

"It is." I nodded and looked around the room. For the first time, I was really seeing the place, and I regretted taking it for granted. How many times had I been at a party like this? Too many times to count. How many times had I disregarded the fact that not everyone lived like this? Too many times to count on that, too. We sat in a room of one percenters, but I'd never thought about them that way before. I'd just let it all drift by me, hardly awake at all. And, if I wanted to be honest with myself, that habit had only grown worse since I'd moved to Palm Beach.

"You're right." I took my water glass off the table and raised it in her direction. "This is something special, and it is high time I stopped forgetting that."

She offered me a smile. "I'm glad I made you think about it."

I was just about to take a sip of water when Aaron caught my eye. He walked toward our table with Maryanne Plunket. When he reached us, his expression softened.

"So glad we could make it," he said as the two of them claimed the open seats next to ours. "Going to be a wonderful night." He extended a hand to Natalie. "I'm Aaron Shields."

Natalie laughed and shook it. "Natalie."

"So, you're the one who's got Luke all tied up in knots."

"Tied up in knots?"

"I'd say so." Aaron laughed at his own comment, then turned to Maryanne. The three of them made small talk. When he finally sat down beside me, he leaned in to my shoulder. "She's hotter than I expected," he said in a low voice.

"As if you're looking."

"I might not be *looking*, but I can still *look*." Aaron clapped me on the bicep. "And she's something."

"I think so, too."

"Did I see your father at Table 10?"

I nodded.

"I thought he hated Palm Beach." Aaron picked up the breadbasket from the table, dug out a pretzel roll, and passed the basket to Maryanne. "He hasn't been here in years."

"I thought so, too. When I told him about the gala last month, he said he wouldn't be able to make it because he had to close a deal in Ireland this week. I had no idea he was coming."

Aaron's nostrils flared. "Interesting."

Our table filled up, and the main program began. Servers presented us kale salads for the first course, while the band played background music from a stage in the center of the room. After the salads, we enjoyed a main course of surf and turf, along with baked potato and more bread. About fifteen minutes later, Grace asked the crowd to give her their attention.

"We're doing a lot of great work here tonight," she said. "I'm happy to say that The Children's Fund Read With America Initiative has raised more than one million dollars this evening, and that those funds will go so far in furthering reading programs for at-risk students across the country. To date, the RWA program is working with two hundred fifty schools along the East and West Coasts. We soon hope to expand those efforts in the Midwest."

The crowd applauded, and she grinned.

"But, I'm also happy to say that we're not done with our efforts this evening. In fact, one of our most generous donors spearheaded the efforts to improve and expand our gala this evening. And I'm happy to say that donor is with us in this room."

My breath caught in my throat. Aaron gave me a nudge.

"Will Mister Luke Rothschild please stand up? Luke, I know you're here, and we can't thank you enough." The crowd began clapping again, and I glanced around the room. Many people were staring at me. Reluctantly, I stood from my chair.

"Ladies and gentlemen, Luke Rothschild is one of our most ardent supporters, and last year, because of him, Read With America expanded to Florida, and into forty-five new schools. Several of those schools have become our most successful, and in one case, a failing school that had a literacy rate of twenty-five percent last year, now has eighty-five percent of students reading at or above grade level." Connie stepped away from the podium and clapped; the rest of the guests followed her lead. "Mr. Rothschild, will you please come forward so that we can formally recognize you?"

I swallowed, plastered a smile on my face, and made my way to the front of the ballroom.

FIFTEEN

Natalie

Everyone else clapped and cheered. I didn't. I sat there in shock. A million dollars raised? *A million?* Responsibility for improving literacy in forty-five Florida schools? Who was this guy?

"Clap, honey," Aaron said over the dull roar of acclimation.

"Right. Of course." I put my hands together, still shocked, and leaned over to him as I began to clap. "I just had no idea he was this generous."

"He is." Aaron lifted one shoulder. "And I tell you this, he won't be happy about this attention. He doesn't like it."

"Why not?"

"Luke prefers to do things in private. Less questions that way. Less to worry about. Just being a Rothschild is a hard enough."

"I can see that," I said, watching as Luke walked up the dais steps and shook hands with Connie. I glanced in the direction of the table where his father and stepmother sat. I couldn't read the expressions on their faces. "It seems like everywhere we go, someone knows him—or thinks that they do."

"And that's only half of it." Aaron laughed. "Not to mention all the pressures. He can never live up to his father's expectations. Never. No matter what he does."

The applause died down. I still felt stunned and overwhelmed as I took in the sight of Luke standing in the center of the podium. Connie handed him the microphone, and he took a deep breath before he addressed the crowd.

"I appreciate the accolades," he said. "But I don't deserve this at all, and I don't seek out this kind of publicity. I just believe in this mission, and I have for a while. And really, tonight isn't about me in any way. It's about all of you—and I want to challenge you to consider over the next few days what you can do to change the outcome for someone in this community. For me, that comes with education."

Luke said a few more words, then gave the microphone back to Connie. When he returned to the table, I couldn't help but stare at him.

"What?" he whispered.

"I didn't expect this," I said as Connie signaled the band and invited the guests to dance. "Not at all."

"I didn't expect it, either." He held out a hand. "Want to dance?"

I tried to bite back a smile, and failed. "What if I say no?"

"Then I'll be devastated."

I took his hand. "Well, we can't have that, can we?"

I didn't have a chance to talk to him about the award until about two hours later, as we drove away from the estate in the McLaren. Once we reached the street, I decided to bring it up. "So that's why they fawned over you at the reception a few weeks ago."

Luke brought the car to a stop at a red light on South County Road. He kept his attention on the street. "Yes."

"You're the biggest supporter they have, aren't you?"

He still didn't look at me. "Yes."

"And for how long?"

The light changed to green. "Long enough."

"And why did you get involved in this?"

"What is this?" He accelerated and began to move the car through the light traffic. "An interrogation?"

"No." I laughed. "Yes. I'm just surprised. You seem really involved in this group, and I just wondered why."

He gave me a sideways glance. "It's complicated."

"I'm sure I can follow."

"When I was a kid, I had trouble reading. A lot of trouble. It wasn't anything that couldn't be fixed, but I was slower. It didn't come easy, and I needed extra help. In fact, I got held back in third grade because I had trouble reading on grade level." Luke laughed to himself. "And trust me, it wasn't the kind of thing my father wanted to deal with; it didn't fit into the kind of story he wanted people to know about our family. A man like him sees his children as assets and his wives as interchangeable. An only son with learning problems didn't fit into his lifestyle. I guess that's the best way to put it."

"Wow."

"We Rothschilds are good at painting a beautiful picture of ourselves, but it's not that great when you get close up."

"But you did get help, right? I mean, you seem fine now."

"Thanks to my mother." Luke pressed the turn signal on the car and changed lanes. "I don't really like talking about it."

"I can tell," I whispered.

He didn't speak again until he stopped the car at another light. "I'm sorry. That was curt. I'm just… sometimes, I still have trouble opening up."

I took his hand. "It's okay."

"Good." He squeezed my palm. "Do you want to come back to my place?"

"Yes." I regarded him. "But only if you tell me about your mom."

He chuckled to himself. "Fair enough. But I'm warning you, Natalie. You might not like what you hear."

"Try me."

"Okay."

The light changed, and Luke drove the car through the intersection.

"She died almost a decade ago." He glanced at me, and our gazes met for a brief second. "The first of two major deaths in my life, and she was a really wonderful person. Shrewd. Knew what she wanted. After she died, my life fell apart, in a way. I didn't handle it well. Then I met Faye, and she died, too…"

"And somehow you ended up here."

"My mother loved Palm Beach. She came here as much as she could, and in the end, she was here almost six months out of the year. I can't blame her for that."

I took his hand. "And because of what you went through, you decided to devote your time to Read With America? That's amazing."

"Plenty of children in our country don't have the advantages that I do, and when I heard about the charity, I decided I'd help any way that I could. Seemed like one way that I could get over my grief."

"Did it help?"

He shrugged.

"You never cease to surprise me, Luke."

He drove the McLaren onto a side street, one that would take us to his oceanfront home. "Same to you, Natalie."

"That was really selfless what you did. A lot of people are going to benefit from your generosity."

"I sure hope so." Luke drove the car into the driveway and cut off the engine. When he turned to me, he narrowed his eyes. "Do you realize how sexy you look in that dress?"

"No." I moved closer to him so that our faces were only inches apart. "I don't think I do."

"Good enough to eat."

The tone of his voice sent a shiver down my spine. I knew what was coming next, and I wanted it—badly. "Well, what are you going to do about that?"

Luke slipped his hand around the nape of my neck and I gave myself over to him. Our lips met, and he kissed me with force, devouring me with his touch. I returned his caresses and our kisses deepened. It didn't take long for something to stir in the deepest part of my body, and he left me breathless with his touch.

"Do you want me here?" I asked when I had the courage to break away. "In the car?"

"No," he murmured. "Upstairs." His forehead touched mine. "I'm going to take you upstairs and make love to you all night. I'm not going to stop until you scream."

"Good," I said. "I expect no less."

The following morning, an incoming call on my phone woke me just before eleven. I rolled over and silenced the ringer, hoping it wouldn't disturb Natalie, who lay naked in the bed beside me. When I saw the name on the phone screen, I let out a soft groan.

No way would I be able to avoid this one. At all.

I tumbled out of bed with the phone in my hand and punched the answer button. Holding it to my ear, I padded into the hallway and asked, "Dad? Is everything all right?"

"Perfectly fine." His deep voice boomed through the receiver. "Why wouldn't it be?"

"Nothing, I..."

Goddamn it, why was I always such a pussy around him? I could be a man about everything else in my life, so why not with him? I shuffled into one of the guest bedrooms I never used and closed the door. "Did you have a nice time last night?"

"I certainly did." He grunted. "And I must admit, I like what I'm seeing from you down here. You're doing great with this Read America deal."

"Read *With* America," I muttered. "And it's an initiative."

"Right. That. I think it's a good place to put some of the foundation's money. We certainly have the room." He paused. "I'd like to see you this afternoon. You and I need to talk about a few things, including your future with our companies."

I winced. Something about his tone of voice had me on edge. He had a way of forcing things and bullying people, even when he wasn't trying to do so, and I felt it through the phone. He wasn't really asking, he was demanding.

"What time?"

"We'll meet in the lobby of The Breakers Resort at one. I already have a reservation."

Not a question, or a request. An order.

"Absolutely," I said. "Looking forward to it."

After our conversation ended, I walked back into my bedroom and took a long look at Natalie. She made my bed better. Simple as that. I wanted nothing more than to wake up next to her—every day.

"Natalie." I moved closer to the bed. "Time to wake up."

She stirred, then stretched. "Hmm. Really?"

"I have to meet with my father, and I can't get out of it," I murmured. "He just called."

"Oh, he did?" She rose up from the bed and rubbed sleep from her eyes. "What time is the meeting?"

"One." I looked down at my Omega watch, which I hadn't bothered to remove from my wrist the night before. "An hour forty-five or so from now. It sounded important."

"I see."

She got out of bed and searched the floor for her clothes, not bothering to hide her naked body. My breath clogged in my throat, and I took in the long, beautiful lines of her torso. When she saw me staring at her, a smile spread across her face. "What?"

"Just thinking about last night." My gaze floated down to the apex of her thighs, then returned to her eyes. "And I'm not talking about the gala."

"Hmm…last night was great, wasn't it?" She strode toward me, letting her handful of clothing fall to her side. Our gazes locked, and stayed that way.

We'd made love three times. Each one was better than the last. And I couldn't remember the last time I'd made love with anyone. For years, I'd only had sex with no emotion. But not anymore.

Natalie reached my side and traced her index finger down the center of my chest. "If you're meeting your dad, you probably need to take a shower."

"I do." I didn't tear my gaze away from her. Couldn't have even if I'd wanted to. I liked that. Wanted more of that. Natalie held my attention more than any other woman I'd ever met.

She rose up on her tiptoes and her lips met mine. "Then let's get you clean," she said after she pecked me on my lips.

We moved farther into the bathroom, and then stepped into the glass-enclosed shower in the far corner of the room. She turned on the water and moved the nozzle to the lukewarm setting. My hands found the gentle curve of her behind, and I pressed up against her.

I was already hard. And ravenous. I lowered my lips to her ear. "Do you know how good you look?"

"*How* good?" She didn't turn around. The steady pulse of the water filled my ears, drowning out everything. There was no one else. Nothing else.

There was only us.

"Good enough to eat," I said, just before I allowed myself to nibble on the nape of her neck. She turned around at the touch of my lips, and her eyes were bright with desire.

"What are you waiting for, Luke? Eat me."

"With pleasure," I said.

I rolled into my father's meeting two minutes late. I didn't need the look on his face to tell me that I'd violated one of his cardinal business rules. He always said that being even a minute late showed disrespect.

"Don't bother with an excuse," he said as I walked through the tall, two-story doors at the entrance to The Breakers property. He stood in the center of the room next to a large mahogany table, covered with an ornate display of flowers that took up most of the surface. Behind him, the Florida sun heated up a sizeable courtyard that linked various wings to the hotel.

"It's complicated," I said. "I really am sorry that I'm late. But you're the one who wanted a spur-of-the-moment appointment."

"I only did that because I can't get you to stay in New York for any decent length of time." As usual, he spoke to me like I was one of the vice presidents in his company, and not like his son. "I have a table in the Circle. Are you eating?"

"Sure," I said. "Sounds wonderful."

As if there was any other way to answer him.

Sunday brunch at The Breakers featured a spread that would have delighted Louis XVII. Eight large buffet sta-tions showcased a full breakfast, salads, made-to-order omelets, prime rib, an endless mimosa bar, a Bloody Mary station, Belgium waffles, sushi, caviar bar, and more. Ta-bles of guests exclaimed over the decadent offerings and dressed-in-resort, chic outfits that blended perfectly with the gold, stucco, and Italian style of the resort.

And any other day, I would have enjoyed my time there. But not that day. That day, I barely noticed any of it. Instead, with every bite of my waffle and every sip of my coffee, I waited for the other shoe to drop. Dad didn't have these kinds of meetings without having something big to discuss.

"As you know, I want to give the company to you," he finally said over a refill of black coffee. "Despite your best efforts to shirk your responsibilities, I think you are the best fit for the business. You're my eldest son. The only person who deserves to succeed me."

"Thank you," I said, keeping my voice even as I racked my brain, trying to think of where this conversation would lead next.

"And that's why I've decided to meet you halfway."

"If this is about that goddamn contract—"

"Forget the contract. I'll have it made null and void when I get back to New York, as long as you agree to help me do what I'm about to propose." He studied me for a beat, and I noticed how much older he appeared. The wrinkles around his eyes had grown deeper, and his sallow skin reminded me of chalk. Time hadn't been on his side, and anyone who saw him would notice that. "For years, I've considered getting back into the South Florida market. I should have done it back in 2009, when no one was buying, but I still think the short-term potential down here isn't over." He cleared his throat. "Especially on the West Palm side of the Intracoastal."

"What kind of potential?"

"Condos, mixed-use developments." He waved his hand. "The kind of thing that appeals to millennials with a little bit of money. I've decided to invest—and invest heavily. I want you to manage this development, and after you're done overseeing it, I'll pass the rest of our assets to you."

Stunned, I sat back in my chair. I hadn't expected this. I hadn't prepared for it. And I didn't know if I really wanted it.

He took his napkin from his lap and backed his chair away from the table. "Are you finished eating?"

"Yes," I croaked.

"Good. I want to show you in person what I'm talking about."

SIXTEEN

Natalie

"*W*hat?"

I looked up from the piece of computer paper, and my gaze met Helen's. Her jaw tightened, and her eyes narrowed.

"No," I said. "You're joking." I placed the printout on the counter of the yoga studio reception desk, which separated us. Then I took a long, hard breath. "This isn't true."

"I wish it wasn't." Helen folded her arms across her chest. "But I checked and then double checked—then checked again. It's legit."

"RCS is an LLC owned by Barrett Rothschild? And he's the one who wants us to close?"

"Yep." Helen elongated the word and slowly nodded her head. "Barrett Rothschild. *Luke Rothschild's father.*"

No, no way. Not the father of the man I wanted to give my heart to—not him.

I must be having a nightmare.

"I can't believe this." My voice trembled as the reality of our situation clattered around in my head.

"Me either." She picked up the paper once again and studied it as if she'd be able to will the facts outlined on it to change. "But here it is. Believe it."

I let out a sigh and glanced around the studio that had become such a centerpiece of both our lives. How much time had we spent here? How many hours had we worked with one goal in mind? How much sweat? How much of my life?

And now, it all threatened to blow away. Just. Like. That.

"I need to tell you something," I said.

Aunt Helen folded the computer paper again and put in on the desk. "Oh? What's that?"

I gulped. Knowing that what I said next wouldn't make her very happy, I still needed to tell her the truth. I wanted to clear it all up between us. She deserved that.

"I've been seeing Luke for the last couple of weeks."

"What?" Helen's eyes widened. "As in, dating?"

"Yeah, people would call it that."

I would have called it even more than that. I was falling for Luke—no, I'd *fallen* for Luke. Hard. Fast. And possibly, forever.

And that made what she'd just told me burn.

"So, you're sleeping with him?"

I swallowed and didn't offer a reply.

"Jesus, Natalie." Helen braced herself against the reception desk. "When were you going to tell me this?"

"There—ugh…just hasn't…I don't…" There it came again, my nervous tic. I couldn't find the words when I needed them. *Damn it.* "I just haven't ever found the right time."

"Never found the right time? Never found the right time? Are you serious? I'm your aunt. *Your family.* And you couldn't find the right way to tell me?" Her voice grew louder with every sentence. "What is this? I thought we didn't have any secrets."

"We don't, it's just that—"

"Who helped you out when you couldn't find a job after graduation? Who made sure you and your mom had extra money when you were growing up? Who was there, babysitting you while your mother worked nights? Me. Always me." Her face flushed, and she took a deep breath. "Do you know how hard that was? I would come home from class at the University of Central Florida, barely have an hour to study, and then spend four nights a week watching you so that my sister could pay her mortgage and keep a roof over your head."

"I know," I whispered.

"You're like a daughter to me, Natalie. I trust you—I trusted you."

"It was just dating—" I said, but every word quivered on my lips. "Nothing."

She regarded me for several long seconds. "No, I don't think it is. I don't think it's 'just dating', is it?"

I bit my bottom lip. "I didn't think you'd understand because…well, I know how it's been the last of couple of months. You've taken things hard. And with all that's happened, all the connections that the Rothschilds have to Wall Street, I just didn't want to go there with you."

"I can't believe this," Helen murmured.

"Everything is so high stakes with you these days. You think everything is a conspiracy."

"No, I don't.

"Yes, you do." I sighed, then looked away from her and fixated on one of the racks of sweatshirts with our logo on them. Another reminder of the things we'd have to get rid of as fast as possible. "And I like Luke. A lot." I shook my head. "Actually, I think I love him."

A moment of silence passed between us.

"Listen, your love life is your business." She covered her face with part of her right hand. "I just...when it comes to the yoga studio, I'm defensive. This is my *baby.*"

"I know."

She rubbed her forehead. "What am I going to do now? Where do I go from here?"

"I could talk to him—to Luke." When she looked up, my gaze met Helen's again. "He could fix this."

"You saw the plans. It's already in the works." She picked up the folded paper and waved it at me. "According to this, it's going to be a signature project for the Roth-schild family. They have millions of dollars tied up in this and it's a huge statement for them." She let out a rueful laugh. "Their reinvestment in the South Florida real estate market."

"There has to be something that can be done. I don't think he knew about this deal."

"How could he not?" She regarded the paper again, then tossed it on a nearby bench. "This is the family business. Emphasis on the word 'family.'"

"I don't know, I just..." The memories of the last days with Luke blurred in my head. Maybe she had a

171

point. I couldn't be sure. "I don't think he'd do something like that. I don't think he'd buy the property and not tell me."

Helen crossed her arms.

"I mean it."

"But if you think about it, you barely know him, Natalie."

She was right. I did barely know him. It had been—what? Two weeks? If that? Sure, I'd slept with him, and we'd shared a few great conversations, but that could mean nothing. And, god, what I'd let him do to me on the bridge...

"What did I tell you about the Rothschilds?" Helen placed her palms on the edge of the reception desk then leaned in to brace her body against it. "They are ruthless. In on everything. Behind everything."

"That's all just internet rumor."

She huffed. "Hardly."

"I thought he was nice," I muttered, still caught up in my own shock. "And last night, he said he'd help us..."

She cocked her head. "Help us?"

"He said he'd pay off all my debts—help us with the closing, all of it. That if we needed money, he'd bail us out."

"Because either way, he wins, right? Since his family owns the development, he's not paying anyone anything." Helen snorted. "He's just paying himself."

We both fell silent and I looked around at the studio again. We didn't have classes that morning, and I gave God a silent "thank you" for that. I still needed time to process everything. And to talk to Luke. Was he done with his meeting, yet?

"We're going to have to…" Her attention turned to something over my shoulder. "Oh, my *god*."

"What?"

"Looks like your boyfriend is here." Her voice dripped with disgust.

"He is?" I spun around in time to see a familiar BMW pull into the parking slot closest to the studio front door. *His* BMW. Luke behind the wheel. And the outline of a man who appeared to be his father in the passenger seat.

"Perfect timing," I said under my breath. "Just perfect."

"I don't want him to come in here." Helen's voice sliced through the stale studio air. "Not right now."

I glanced at her. "I don't think we have a choice."

Luke was already opening the car door.

Luke

I should have seen this coming. "Should" being the operative word. If I wanted to be honest, I should have seen a lot of things coming. A lot. But I didn't. It was only when my father directed us into the shopping center parking lot that I realized the true scope of his plan.

"This is it?" I slowed the car as we signaled to enter the lot. "*This* is the construction site?"

He shrugged. "If you want to call it that. Twenty-five thousand square feet of dilapidated space. Perfect for a development like this." He surveyed the property, then pointed at a few bare trees in a distant landscape divider. "We have interest from several national chains for a new-concept grocery store that I think we can place over there. Above it, we'll sell about five floors of luxury apartments with a rooftop pool. I already have an architect designing a few water features…"

"Stop it."

He recoiled. "Stop what?"

"You know what. *This*." I slowed the car a little bit more, keeping Natalie and Helen's yoga studio in my sights as the car drew closer to the open spots in front of the business. "We don't need to do this."

"Do what?"

I parked the car and turned off the engine. "Develop here. Take over a random shopping center."

"Of course, we do. We need to make a statement in the South Florida market, and I can't think of a better way to do it. Since you insist on living here, this can be your pet project. Consider it a statement of confidence about you and your…decisions."

"But I—"

"Don't interrupt me, son. Granted, this 'random' shopping center has seen far better days. Which is why we're doing the city of West Palm Beach a favor. The whole area needs a new look, and together, we're going to bring it."

I regarded him for a breath, then turned back toward the studio in time to see Natalie striding through the front door. A large frown marred her beautiful face. Did she know what I knew? Did she realize?

I locked my gaze on hers. Fiery. Her eyes were balls of fire.

Yep, she did know, all right.

Shit.

"Oh," my father said. "I see. That's the woman you brought to the gala, isn't it?"

"Yes."

He glanced from me, to her, and a back again. "She's wearing a studio shirt, and she looks like an employee." He sniffed. "Luke, does she *work* here?"

I set my jaw and didn't answer.

"Luke, answer me." He sighed. "Or maybe you don't need to. I'm sure I can guess."

"She's a great person, Dad." I turned to him. "And she makes me feel something that I haven't felt in a long time. Something I didn't even feel with Faye."

He narrowed his eyes. "With a body like that, I can imagine she does."

"Don't talk about her like that!" I slammed the palm of my hand into the car steering wheel. "Do not. You don't get to say things like that about her."

"I'm going to overlook the fact that you conveniently left out important details about this woman, like where she works, when you introduced us last night."

I couldn't remember a time when my father had sounded so cold and unfeeling. He was dead inside—but I wasn't. I had never been more alive, and it wasn't because of the anger I felt about what he'd just said. It was because of the love I felt for her.

"You don't even know her." I gritted my teeth. "She's a good person."

"That may be, but I know enough to know that this woman isn't right for you, son. She won't be an asset to our family. Sometimes, you can tell that just by looking at a person."

I grunted and stepped foot out of the car. I didn't have time to think about him. I needed to focus on her. Needed to explain this to her. And I needed to figure a way out of this.

"I would say I'm surprised to see you, but I'm not," she said, not bothering to greet me as I got out of the car. I didn't have to guess any more. She knew. No question.

"I can explain." I slammed the door shut, leaving my father inside the BMW. He didn't try to get out. Thank god. "This isn't…"

"What is this?" She held up a piece of computer paper, but she didn't give me the time to see it or to answer her. "Never mind. *I'll* tell you what this is! It's an article announcing a new development, and it outlines your father's plan to 'revitalize' the area. What the hell?"

"It's something he cooked up. Something my father decided to do, one of his 'big ideas.'"

"With you, right?" She glanced at the article. "That's what it says here. That he bought this development with your permission. Your input. It says this is going to be a father-and-son venture, and that you've both been working on this for months. *Months*." Natalie shook her head. "When were you going to tell me?"

"I swear—I didn't know anything about this until the meeting this morning. I had no idea what he planned for this development. I'm serious. No clue."

She crossed her arms and it crushed the paper. Fitting. "Somehow, I find that hard to believe. This is the family business. Your business."

"No, it's not. It hasn't been for a while." I glanced back at the car. My father still sat in the passenger seat, watching us argue on the sidewalk in front of her aunt's business. "I've barely had anything to do with my father's company for the last two years. You know that."

"Pfffftttt. No, I don't."

"I'm serious."

"Helen was right." She narrowed her eyes, and I guessed she was hearing my words, but not listening. "Damn it. She was."

"What makes you say that?"

"She warned me about you and your family. She said this"—she sliced a hand through the air—"whatever this was, wasn't all that it seemed. That it *never* is when it comes to your family. If you all can't profit from it, then you're not interested."

"You know it's not like that. Not with you, babe, not—"

I tried to speak further, but she held up a hand to stop me. "Please, don't say anything more." Her voice cracked. Somehow, the fire had been sucked out of her in an instant, only to be replaced by uncertainty and pain. "D-don't make excuses. J-just don't."

I cleared my throat, fighting the urge to yank her into my arms and soothe the sudden anguish dulling her pretty eyes. "But I think if you could just give me a chance to explain…"

"Leave." Her voice became a raspy whisper. "Now."

"Natalie—"

She shook her head, causing one lone tear to spill over her cheek.

My own eyes stung when her teardrop dripped onto the paper she held close to her chest. *To hell with it. To hell with Dad. I needed Natalie in my arms, in my* life. I swore under my breath and took a step toward her, my arms open, ready to take her into my world.

She shifted her worried gaze toward her aunt's yoga studio and I caught a gleam of loyalty and love for family there. I admired that in her, even envied it, envied that I couldn't have that with my father.

She stumbled backward. "Luke, did you hear what I said? Just go."

"But, Natalie, I told you… I didn't know about this until this morning when—"

She crossed her arms and stared at the sidewalk. "Please. I can't do this anymore," she whispered.

I studied every saddened yet determined nuance about her for what felt like eons, and I wondered what this was. Was this a breakup? Goodbye? What was this? Was this all about loyalty to her aunt, or was she really done with me?

My world turned gray, dismal, but I knew what I had to do.

"Okay," I finally said. "If that's what you want, I will. I'll go."

SEVENTEEN

Luke

“**Y**ou have to understand something, son. It's just business. Nothing more,” dad said as I drove us back towards Palm Beach. “And you can't make business personal. When you start adding emotion to it, you get burned. I've always tried to teach you that.”

“Stop,” I muttered before turning to him. “You have no heart, do you?”

“What are you talking about?”

“Your empire. It has consumed you.”

My father shook his head. “I hardly think that's an accurate description of me. I work hard. I built a great company from nothing. And now we are going to take it to the next level. South Florida is a great place to invest right now, and we absolutely don't want to miss out on it.”

“Something you are willing to do at any cost.”

"Certainly. At any cost." The corners of his mouth turned down. "Jesus, you've done exactly what I warned you to never do, haven't you? You've fallen for that yoga instructor. *A nobody*."

I grunted.

"As if I need to ask any more." His voice turned sharper and he settled back into his seat. "A yoga instructor. Of all people."

"That's just it," I said. "She's not 'just' a yoga instructor. She's—she's a better person than I'll ever be. Did you know that she saved a homeless person's life the other night?" I looked over at my father, and the anger I felt towards him threatened to spill over into rage. He simply didn't get it, and for Christ sakes, I knew right then that he never would. "She has a good heart, and she's not driven by the hollowed out, empty things that you are."

Fuming, I focused back on the road and tried to concentrate on driving. It didn't work very well.

"Remember, Luke, you're a *Rothschild*. We are one of the most storied families in the country. And that aerobics instructor—"

"Yoga. Not aerobics. Yoga. And she has a name." I flipped the turn signal as we approached the next four-way intersection. When the light changed from red to green, I drove us back on the bridge toward Palm Beach. "Maybe not a name you recognize, but a name."

"Think about it, son, how will this look?"

"Her name is Natalie Johnson."

"I don't care what her name is," he grumbled. "I don't have to know it to know that she doesn't fit."

"Oh, really?"

"No, she doesn't, and I'm certain she never will." He gripped my shoulder and I moved out from underneath his hold. He sighed. "You can be pissed off at me all that you want, but it's the truth, and you can't get away from it. You're the scion of the Rothschild family. *My first born.* You have duties that you can't escape. One of those is that the company I built is your birthright. The other is that you need to make sure we live on—that we don't become one of those families that fades away. We've been in this country for over four hundred years, and always at the top. I'm not about to let you tear that down."

"But I—"

"No, Luke!" He pounded his fist on the dashboard. "You don't get to destroy us."

"Us? Since when is this about us? It's always only ever been about you."

"Come on, you know that's not true."

"Yes, it is, Dad. You don't want to admit it, but it is." I maneuvered the car onto the bridge, silently counting the seconds until we'd get back to The Breakers and I could put distance between my father and myself. "This is always about you. Money. Prestige. The three things you love the most."

"If you don't take on this development with me, Luke, there will be no turning back."

I frowned and stared at his faceless expression for a long moment. He'd said this sentence so clinically, as if he'd completely divorced himself from me. "What do you mean?"

"I'll be forced to implement the alternative." He waved a hand. "Delay my retirement. Place your brother in line as the main heir."

"My *half*-brother."

"Whatever you choose to call him. I don't want to do this, but I'm losing my patience. Besides, Marcus is a very bright student." His mouth twisted into a half-smile. "And perhaps I can make it work with him."

"Sounds like you want that more than you're willing to admit."

"I want someone willing to make hard decisions. Someone who won't let emotions get in the way of a good deal. You've always had trouble with that, Luke. It has always been one of your weakest traits." His tone softened. "Come on, son, I know you. You're part of me. We're the same. This isn't something you want to turn down. Imagine all we can achieve."

I sighed. "I need time to think."

We drove the rest of the way home in silence. As we approached the valet drop-off, he turned to me again. "Listen, Lenora and I are leaving town in the morning. I want your answer before we go."

"Answer?"

"You're either a Rothschild, or you aren't. Simple as that." He cleared his throat. "You either join the project, or you're out of the family. For good." He opened the car door and stepped out of my BMW. "I'll give you some time to consider everything. But as I said, I expect to hear your final answer tomorrow. We're departing Palm Beach International at eight."

After I dropped my father off at the resort, I returned home and wandered around my beach house. I had to admit it—I'd relied on the Rothschild name for everything I had. What would it be like if I didn't have it to back me up? What would that life look like? Could I make it on my own?

Maybe.

It wouldn't be pretty or make me comfortable, but I could do it. I had a degree, and decent business background. I knew more about life than my father gave me credit for, and on top of that, I had common sense.

Even better—I knew I didn't want to let the one decent thing that had happened to me in years walk away.

Sitting in the study about a half hour after the confrontation at the yoga studio, I placed a call to Aaron. He picked up on the first ring. "Luke, what a surprise! Up for a round of golf later this week?"

"No, I won't be able to make it." I sank into the blue leather armchair located in the corner of the library. "Listen, if I needed to liquidate my holdings, how much could I get a hold of, and how long would it take?"

"Are we talking the full amount or—"

"My accounts. What I own outright, and independent of the Rothschild holdings."

Aaron let out a whistle. "You know that's less than thirty percent of your net."

"I do." I rubbed my brow, aware I was asking him for something he never thought he'd hear. "But that's the figure I need."

Aaron didn't reply for a beat. When he did, he croaked out the words. "What is this about? It sounds serious, man."

"In a way, it is."

Aaron cleared his throat. "Meaning…?"

"Earlier this month, you mentioned that hedge fund had done pretty well." I tapped my fingers on the armchair. "Where are we now with that?"

"I haven't checked the balance in a few days, but it looked good last week, and the market has been up lately." He paused. "Do you mind if I ask why you want to know? You never care about things like this."

"Just give me a ballpark. I know it's a lot less than it was when I first came to you—"

Aaron laughed without humor. "I've never seen someone spend money the way that you do. Are you thinking about getting another car? Maybe a vintage one?"

"No." I sat up straighter in the chair and chose my next words very carefully. "This time it involves my future. My future with Natalie."

"I see." He made a clicking sound with his mouth. "It would take a little while, but I can get a number to you this afternoon."

"Perfect," I said. "Why don't you bring over a report this evening?"

"I'll have something ready around seven."

EIGHTEEN

Natalie

I didn't know what to think. Didn't know what to feel. Didn't know how to process any of what I'd just learned. I was sad. Incredulous. Disappointed. In shock.

"I need to go home," I told Helen just moments after Luke and his father drove away. "I can't—I'll call you later. I need a little while to deal with this."

"But we…we must come up with a plan for winding down the business," she said, the words leaving her mouth hard and fast. "What are we—well, what am *I*—going to do? I have less than thirty days to come up with a solution."

"I know," I said. "I'll call you later. I promise. We will get through this."

I couldn't even remember how I got home, but somehow, I made it to the parking lot of my apartment complex. I sat in the car for a few minutes, staring into space as I tried to process the reality of what had just happened. What had I been thinking? Luke and I came from different worlds, and there was no denying that. He had family commitments, a name, and a business putting pressure on him. I had none of that, and nothing to offer him. We'd never fit. This would never work.

Sometimes, reality just had to be faced.

I found my way into my second-floor apartment and located a bottle of whiskey in the kitchen cabinet. I couldn't remember who'd given it to me as a college graduation gift, but I'd promised myself I'd save it for an emergency.

No time like the present—which qualified as an emergency.

I poured half a can of diet soda into a plastic glass and topped it off with a generous serving of the liquor. "Bottoms up," I said to no one. Then I swallowed a third of the drink in one large gulp. It felt smooth. Crisp. Like an escape.

And god, I needed it.

Bang. A pause. *Bang. Bang.*

"Natalie?" a muffled voice said. "Are you in there? Natalie."

I opened my eyes. Somehow, I'd made it to the couch and lay there, sprawled across the cushions. Everything seemed foggy. I stared at the door. How long had I been asleep?

"Natalie?" The person on the other side of the door knocked a few more times. "I saw your car in the parking lot."

Recognizing the voice, I sat up from the sofa. Luke. What was he doing here? I glanced at the clock above the stove in the galley kitchen. It read 9:45 PM.

Wow, I've been asleep a long time…

"Give me a minute," I called toward the door. My voice sounded like I had a half-dozen cotton balls in my mouth.

"Okay," Luke said through the door.

I rushed into the bathroom, located in the short hallway between the living room and bedroom of my apartment. The alcohol had done its work. A haggard, pale, still halfway drunk woman stared back at me in the mirror. I splashed some water on my face, wiped my lips with a tube of Black Honey I found in the medicine cabinet, pinched my cheeks, and wrestled my hair into a topknot on my head.

When I opened the apartment front door, I found Luke on the other side with one arm propped against the doorframe. His handsome, flushed face didn't hide anything.

"What are you doing here?" I asked.

"We need to talk, Natalie. Can I come in?"

I shrugged and stepped aside. In all honesty, I still felt too drunk to care about having Luke Rothschild inside my meager apartment. It had been a long day. Long week.

The perfect time to start giving zero fucks.

"What do you want?" I asked again after I closed the door. "If this is about the eviction—"

He held up a hand. "Just give me a chance to explain."

"I don't know if I want to." I leaned against the door and didn't bother crossing the room. If Luke noticed, it didn't show on his face. Instead, he settled onto the left side of my shabby red couch and placed a manila file folder on the cushion beside him.

"I can only guess what you must think of me. What you must think of the last few weeks."

I closed my eyes. "I have a few opinions."

"This is not what you think."

I opened my eyes. "What do you mean? Seems pretty clear to me."

He tilted his head, giving me his full attention.

"I've been thinking this over." I let out a long, heavy breath. "And no matter what—not matter how hard we try, we can't overcome the one thing that will always keep us apart." I rubbed a hand over my face. "We are from two different worlds."

It surprised me how detached I managed to sound as I made this argument to Luke. Maybe the cocktail had been a better friend than I'd expected.

"Being from two different worlds has never stopped us before," he said, his voice even, steady, and calculating. "It doesn't have to stop us now."

I shrugged. I wasn't following him. "How?"

As our gazes locked, Luke's eyes softened around the edges. "I don't care about being a Rothschild anymore, Natalie. It doesn't matter to me." He tapped the manila folder. "And I realized this afternoon, I don't *have* to care. Not anymore. My father doesn't own me."

"But what about the contract?

He stood from the couch. As he said his next words, he took a few tentative steps toward me. "It doesn't matter to me anymore. My father can take his company and all he has with it." He paused. "I'm leaving it all behind. For good."

NINETEEN

Luke

Natalie's eyes bulged, and her mouth dropped open. She closed it and gulped. "What?"

"You heard me loud and clear. I'm leaving the company for good. Permanently. No questions asked, no turning back. I'm giving up my place as the heir to the Rothschild fortune." I stopped a few inches away from her—close, but not too close. "I don't need it. I'm walking away from all of it."

"You are?"

I nodded. "Effective tomorrow morning." Then I laughed. The decision to take this leap felt so liberating, so true. It might have been the first real thing I'd ever done. "In fact, I never really did need it."

"You're kidding."

"Nope." I squeezed her shoulder. "I wouldn't joke about something like this. You might not believe me, but I wouldn't lie to you. I never have, and I never will. I am deadly serious."

She frowned. "You're telling me that you're willing to walk away from a ten-billion-dollar fortune." She swallowed again. "*Ten billion.*"

The way Natalie said the word "ten billion" reminded me just how much money I'd decided to leave behind, and she was right. It was more money than most people could fathom. Still, I didn't care.

"Money isn't everything." With my thumb, I pointed behind my shoulder at the blue folder on the couch "Besides, I think I found a workaround."

"You did?"

I moved my hand from her shoulder and traced her hairline, pushing a few wayward strands away from her face. "You want to have a seat and hear me out on this one?"

She bit her luscious bottom lip and stared at me for a moment before nodding. "Okay." She moved away from the door and took a seat on the couch. "I'm listening."

"What I'm about to tell you, I haven't told anyone." I took a deep breath as I regarded the woman across the room from me. I had her full attention. "Over the last few years, I've done a decent job of saving money and living below my means—despite what it looks like on the outside. I've socked money away."

Natalie settled further into the sofa. I couldn't tell what she was thinking, but I could hope.

"I never had any idea what I'd do with the money, but now I know." Keeping my gaze on her, I picked up the folder and opened it. "I have a hundred thousand in liquid cash and another two hundred fifty grand in a brokerage funds that Aaron set up for me a few years ago. Lately, the market has been…good." I glanced down at the first paper in the folder, a graph of the assets I'd printed just before driving to her apartment. "I also have some fine art at the house worth about fifty grand, and I think I can get a buyer for the McLaren." I looked up at Natalie again. "In all, about four hundred thousand. And I think it's enough. More than enough."

"What are you saying?" she whispered.

"I can pay off your debt. All of it…we can start over. Together. Just us. Free and clear."

Natalie's body suddenly started trembling. She got to her unsteady feet and stumbled into a graceless, backward spider walk across the couch until she found herself against the molding that rimmed the small opening between the living room and kitchen of the apartment. "T-together? W-walk away?"

"Yes." I followed her. "No one has ever made me feel the way that you do. No one. You stir emotions I never thought I had." I grasped her hand and glanced down at her quivering fingers, which had entwined with mine. "And even your cute little nerves are worth it. *You're* worth it, baby."

"Y-you'd give it all up—b-b-billions with a capital B—just for *me*?"

"We'll have enough money to open up a new yoga studio. A chain of them, if you want," I teased with a smile. "So, what are you waiting for? Say yes."

"Your father will never agree to this, Luke. You're his son. His heir."

"I've never been what my father wanted. And he has Marcus to give the company to." I trailed my free hand up her leg. "So, what are you waiting for? Say yes."

She stared at me for a long moment. I tried to read her expression, tried to get a handle on her thoughts. Would she agree? Did she understand what I was offering her? She had to…

"But I could never do that," she finally said. "I can't take money from you. It's not right."

"You're not taking, and it's not a gift. It's a partnership. Us. Together." I tightened my hand on her knee. "I never wanted anything until I met you. I took it all for granted. But now… I can't stand it if you're not in my life, Natalie. *I have to have you.*"

"But how would we—?"

"You can bring Helen into it." I stood, and pulled her up with me. The folder fell to the floor, but I disregarded it for a moment. "I don't care. We'll do franchises. Whatever you want…we can…just say yes." I wrapped my hands around her upper arms. "Say you'll do it—with me."

"You really mean this, don't you?"

"Every word," I whispered.

She furrowed her brow, and then a smile crept across her face. "A partnership, huh?"

"Whatever you want." Keeping my gaze on hers, I leaned forward and put my forehead against hers. "But I haven't heard you say yes yet."

She laughed once. "Yes. Yes, Luke Rothschild. Yes!"

My lips found hers and I pulled her toward me. I tasted everything in her kiss—the promise of the future, a chance at something new, and a love I'd never allowed myself to feel. I had it. I'd come home. I was finally whole.

EPILOGUE

Natalie

Eighteen Months Later

"How many people do we have signed up now?" Luke asked as he emerged from the men's changing room at Namaste Now of Palm Beach Gardens. He carried a stack of fluffy white towels.

"Fifty-six." I glanced at the computer screen, which showed me a layout of the cycling studio that made up the back part of the franchise. Only four bikes remained open, and we had an hour to go until our first class at that location. "We're going to sell out the bikes."

"Fantastic, honey." He placed the towels in the large rattan cubicle that sat next to Namaste Now apparel we had for sale in the front of the store. A few months ago, Helen had designed custom tanks, t-shirts, leggings, hats, and sweatshirts with Namaste Now's intricate, scripted design. We had trouble keeping them in stock.

195

Luke walked around the racks of clothing, making sure they were all perfect, before he spoke to me again. "See? What did I tell you, Natalie?" He winked. "A premium cycling and yoga studio is just what this part of South Florida needed. Aren't you glad I come up with such fantastic ideas?"

"Not like you don't jump at all the chances to remind me whenever you can." I closed Namaste Now's email account, locked the computer screen, and walked around the large reception desk. When I reached Luke, I braced my hand on the metal frame holding half a dozen grey pullover sweatshirts. "We're on our third location. I'd think you could give that up by now."

He spread one hand. "What can I say? I'm a Rothschild, remember? Being a business genius runs in the family."

"Okay, I'll give you that. You're still horrible at hot yoga, though."

He chuckled. "One of the million reasons why I still need you around."

"Yep, you do." I took his hand in mine, and the fire of that contact still felt as warm as it had the first time he'd touched me. How lucky had I been in life? I was one of the luckiest women on earth. I had a great guy who'd given up everything for me, and a business that was finally turning a profit instead of sucking me dry. "But I will give you this—you're great at taking risks."

"Taking risks is the best part of life." Luke leaned in and kissed me. "But the best risk I ever took was the one I took on you. On *us*."

And the thing of it was—he was right.

ACKNOWLEDGEMENTS

This book would not have been possible without the hard work of many wonderful people. Thank you to all the early beta readers of this work, along with Lauren, Josie, Kevin, Ainsley, Judi, Julie, Jenny, and Sean. You all make my world go 'round! Thank you for supporting something that has always been a dream for me. I wouldn't be able to pursue any of this without your immense help and support.

OTHER BOOKS BY SARA CELI

CPSIA information can be obtained
at www.ICGtesting.com
Printed in the USA
FSHW010504040919
61694FS